THE BILLIONAIRE AND THE VIRGIN

ANGEL DEVLIN

CHAPTER ONE

H

June 2004

"Henry, when can I take this blindfold off? I swear I'll trip over in a minute and squash the baby."

"A few more steps, honey, and there's no way I'm going to let you do anything that will harm a hair on either yours or our son's head."

I guided her further from the car down to the driveway until Veronica faced the door.

"Ready?" I asked. "I'm going to remove the

blindfold, so it might take a moment to adjust to the light."

"Hurry, Henry. I'm so goddamn excited."

I removed the blindfold and my wife gasped. In front of her was the front door of a nine-bed house in East Hampton. She took a few steps back and swung around, taking in the enormous yard, then back to the front of the house. She was yet to notice the separate three-bed annex and when we eventually walked through the house, she'd see there was a pool house to the rear.

"Henry, what is this?" She asked. My wife was always cautious, she never assumed anything, never took anything for granted.

"This, honey," I replied, taking her in my arms and stroking her honey-blonde hair, "is our new family home. That's if it meets your approval once we've been inside."

"But, it's so huge. There's only the two of us..." She placed her hands across her stomach, "For another five months, anyhow."

I kissed the top of her forehead. "Our son is just the start. Let's see how many of the rest of the seven guest bedrooms we'll be able to fill."

She laughed at that. Her green eyes glistened with unshed tears. The baby hormones had been making her very emotional of late. "You'd better take me inside to look at it then," she moved out of my arms and grabbed my hand instead.

I took her through every room one by one. Through the living room with its vast windows that flooded the room with light, with sea-blue couches reminding us that the beach was only a few minutes away. An archway led through to a dining room, with a mirror-topped table that seated ten, and then through again to a magnificent white kitchen. But of course, what I was now desperate to show her was our master suite—a large room painted white, with floor-to-ceiling windows adjacent to patio doors that led out onto our own private balcony with a stunning view of the ocean.

"Henry, this is too much."

"Vee, we came from nothing. Built ourselves up from rock bottom, worked our asses off, and now we get to enjoy the benefits of our investments paying off."

"I guess so," she looked out at the view. "And it sure is pretty. We get WiFi here okay though, don't we?"

"Yes, my workaholic wife. You'll be able to run your property empire from whichever room in the house you decide to turn into your office."

"I like to keep busy." She said and then she clutched her head. "Ooooh." She gripped my arm. "Wow, that hurt."

"You okay?" I led her to the edge of the bed. Vee had always suffered with tension headaches, an unfortunate side effect of the stresses of running a billion dollar business, but the last couple of days she'd been complaining more.

"I'm going to ring Dr. Anderson later." I told her. "It could be due to your blood pressure."

"You fuss too much." She said. "I'm just going to freshen up in the bathroom. I'll be right back."

"You sure you're fine?" I asked again and was given a narrow-eyed glare. I raised my hands in surrender. "Backing off."

"Good." She smiled. "I love you, Henry Carter, but I'm an independent woman and I can splash water on my face all by myself."

"I can't wait for you to see the bathroom." I said. It was enormous with a free-standing bath and separate steam room amongst other luxuries.

Vee had been in the bathroom for a few minutes when I called out to check she was okay. Yes, I fussed; yes, she could just get used to it. When there was no response, I hurried over to the room, fully expecting her to chastise me once again for fussing.

But she didn't.

My beautiful wife was slumped on the floor.

I'd not heard her fall because the house was so damn large.

They told me afterward that even if I had heard her, I'd have been too late. An undiagnosed brain tumor had taken my beautiful wife. Our baby boy died too inside his mother's womb at eighteen weeks old.

I lost my wife.

I lost my son.

I lost my ability to love.

My world was gone and with it went my hopes and dreams.

Instead of celebrating life, we mourned the death of a woman taken too soon, and that of my son, taken before he even had the chance to take an independent breath.

I stood at the graveside with Vee's mother, father, stepfather, and her young stepsister. Amelia was just nine years old and spent the entire funeral inconsolable, wrapped in the arms of her parents. I stood beside Vee's father, who'd never remarried after separating from her mother.

"I'll never love anyone else." I told him.

"We'll understand if you do." He said, then he looked at his ex-wife, "But I never did."

I put the house straight back on the market and sold it to the first people who offered on it. I didn't give a damn what I got for it, I just needed it gone.

I kept the business going. I owed it to my beautiful wife to work my ass off to keep our property empire growing.

Years passed.

I had needs.

I visited a sex club, and I had my needs met, with no strings.

Never again would I marry or try for a family.

I bought the club and named it Club S.

Everyone thought Club S stood for Club Sex.

It didn't.

It stood for Club Stop. It was where I called time on my life.

CHAPTER TWO

H

Club S. A place of drunken debauchery. A place where I could seek pleasure with no pressure. To everyone there I was H. It had been a long time since I'd been Henry.

The club was decorated in black tones alongside silver accents. Sleek and dark, rather like myself. The people who worked and played there may have thought they knew me, but they didn't. Only one woman had gotten close a couple years ago. Her name had been Tiffany. What had started out as a pleasurable fuck had become something more. I'd begun to care. But I couldn't love her, didn't love her, and in the end she married someone else. The fact was I'd arranged for her to meet her future husband. I'd arranged for him to move into the apartment next door to hers. Of course, I hadn't known then she would marry him. It was a pleasing outcome and freed me to return to what I'd done before—join in the scenes at my club.

At Club S there were rooms where almost anything went. There was also a stage you could hire in advance, or, if it wasn't booked, you could bid on the stage in an evening and act out your desires in front of an audience. I'd very rarely been front of stage, preferring to choose a beautiful conquest in the other rooms.

Often, Aidan Hall would join me. A wealthy businessman like myself, Aidan had been begging me to sell him the club for the last year. He wanted to expand and had recently bought an adult film company, GoDown Films. He thought Club S fit into his portfolio nicely, and over the last month or so, his bargaining had stepped up a pace. For the last few years, Aidan had sometimes joined me in a ménage. It was only to please women, neither of us were interested in male to male, but sometimes it helped to have a partner to make a woman's fantasies come true.

Tonight was no exception. Having enjoyed a few

scotches at the bar, I moved into the rooms, nodding at the doorman as I went past. I accepted the black wristband with silver stars that showed I was ready to join in the fun, and I mingled amongst the voyeurs. The rooms had large windows, and some members liked only to observe, identified by a white wristband. The rooms could be closed off or opened up, anything really as long as it was consensual. Today had been a fraught business day. I'd had a lot of properties to purchase and manage, and I really needed to employ another member of staff, or let some business go. I could even retire! Maybe I should consider selling Club S at some point? The fact was I was thirty-eight years old and didn't know what the fuck to do with my life anymore. I was just going through the motions. The only thing I got satisfaction from these days was fucking and even that was getting old.

I wondered what life would have been like if Vee had lived. How many kids would we have had? Would we have given up the businesses to care for our family? I already knew the answer to that one deep down. Vee had been a career woman. She'd have loved our kids with all her heart, but she'd needed to work; she'd thrived on the buzz of a deal. We'd made a fabulous team. I shook my head to bring myself back to the present time. The scotch had hit and diluted the barrier I placed across my mind, the one that kept trying to tell me that Vee was becoming a ghost wife now, from a time before that now seemed like a different lifetime. It became harder each day to picture her face and to remember our times together. It's not true that time healed, it's just it made it difficult to remember.

I looked through a viewing window and found Aidan there with his cock in a redhead's mouth. She had a pixie crop and looked eager to please. Aidan gave an almost imperceptible nod, and I entered the room.

I slipped off my shoes, shed my black pants and jacket, unbuttoned my shirt, and then removed everything else until I was completely naked.

I was more than comfortable with my body and judging by how the pupils of the redhead's eyes had just dilated, she was happy I was there too. I stood running a hand up and down my ten-inch cock. Aidan wasn't small, but I had a couple of inches on him and I was ready to let 'Red' enjoy them.

Aidan slipped out of her mouth and nodded towards me. Red crawled across the floor to me and then took me in her warm mouth. God, I loved the sensation of a warm mouth around my cock and I loved it even more when I thrust myself further into a willing woman's throat so that drool dribbled down their chin as they tried to manage me. I held onto the back of her head as I felt my cock hit the back of her throat. She handled everything I gave her, no innocent to the act of giving head. That was the thing here at the club most of the time, the people who were members tended to love sex and not get enough of what they wanted in the outside world. It was rarely an innocent person who came to Club S. We had a healthy membership, but I knew that whereas I had kept the business small, Aidan wanted to relaunch, rename, and put the place on the map, with a view to expansion across different cities. Once again, I wondered if it was time to let a younger man take the reins and put myself out for retirement. I wasn't old myself, just jaded and in need of something new in my life, though what that was I had no idea.

I realized I'd become lost in thought while Red was sucking my dick. Was I becoming so desensitized to the club that even this wasn't doing it for me anymore? I couldn't look Red in the eyes. I withdrew my cock, turned her over onto all fours, and slammed my cock into her wet heat, making her groan with lust. Aidan thrust his cock back into her mouth and we spit-roasted her. I held onto her hips, driving my cock in her as Aidan cupped and squeezed her breasts. As the pressure built up inside me, I slipped a finger onto her clit and caressed her there until she began to come, the tremors from her orgasm milking my cock. As I reached my own climax, I withdrew my cock and let my silky, sticky stream hit the globes of her white ass. Then I left the room just as Aidan released his own cum right down Red's throat.

I wiped myself on a towel at the edge of the room and dressed quickly. I'd come and yet had gained no satisfaction mentally from the act I'd just been involved in. It wasn't working anymore. Being honest, it was becoming as boring as answering emails. Just another job. Yes, my cock thanked me for my efforts, but my mind yelled its frustration.

We didn't want Red.

We didn't want to have sex at the club anymore.

We're bored, Henry.

G reat, I was having mental conversations between my brain and my dick. I really was screwed in a bad way.

. . .

I left the club and headed on home.

My driver Matthew pulled up outside the house and I let myself into my apartment. Mary, my housekeeper, had left me a note letting me know where the food she'd prepared for me was and how to reheat it. She'd written a whole host of other things, but I had no time to read an essay right now. I'd realized how hungry I was. I would starve to death without her. She had been with me for over ten years now and as the mother of four daughters had at first tried to get me interested in them, bringing them by the apartment with the most stupid excuses until finally they'd all got married and settled down. Then a sadness had come over her that always underlaid her expression. She mothered me, even though I had parents of my own, albeit on the other side of the world. But part of her personality had dulled when she hadn't been able to fix me.

I heated up the mac and cheese she'd left for me and sat against the kitchen island to tuck into it, grabbing some crusty bread from the bowl she'd left. As I reached to bring her note closer to me on the countertop, so I could read the rest of what she'd put, I heard a banging noise, like a door opening or closing.

Fuck. Was someone in my apartment?

Footsteps made their way nearer to where I was. Had Mary not left after all? But why would she still be here? I quickly scanned the note from after the part where Mary had talked about mac and cheese.

So, what a surprise today. Why didn't you tell me we were expecting a guest? I had to hurry to get the room all ready for her. My, she's a sweet thing. A lot different I should expect from when you last saw her. And I'm going to be telling you off for that. Amelia says she hasn't seen you in fourteen years!

Amelia?

Little Amelia is here?

I jumped off my stool as the door to the kitchen opened and stupidly I expected to see a young girl, my last faded memory being of someone I barely knew being consoled by her parents at my dead wife's graveside.

But that's not who came through the door.

A tall, slim woman with golden-blonde long hair, and endless legs is what careered through the door. She was dressed in a short suit with sneakers on her feet. As she saw me, she ran and threw her arms around me. All I noticed was that those small pert breasts I glimpsed the shape of through that top were now crushed against my chest. Her arms were around me and her hair was under my nose. She smelled of vanilla.

"Henry. Jeez, man. It's been years."

I held her back at arms-length and took in her appearance, trying to find some resemblance to Vee, or some hint of the little girl from the graveside, but there was nothing. Just a perfect stranger in front of me.

"Amelia?"

"Yes, it's me. Guess I've changed a little, huh? Now why don't you fix us both a coffee or open some wine, and I'll tell you why I'm here. I hope it's not a bad surprise? I figured you'd have space for a guest for a night, and Mary said it would be okay?"

She spoke so fast I could barely keep up with her conversation, what with my trying to process that she was here— both in Manhattan and in my apartment—and why she would be here. Opening wine sounded like the best idea so far and so I busied myself, choosing a nice bottle of red and locating two glasses. Amelia hopped on a stool at the kitchen island like she had lived her for years, and bemused I joined her sitting on an adjacent stool.

I passed her a glass and ran a hand through my hair.

"So, Amelia. What brings you to Manhattan?"

"Truth?"

I nodded.

"I was so damn bored. My parents just spend all their time at The Hamptons and I need more from life. I'm twenty-three now. I want a career and I want to live in Manhattan."

"And you thought I could help you with those things?" I gave her a small smirk as I had no idea what was going through this young woman's mind.

"Oh God no. I was going to rent a small apartment for a while until I got on my feet, but Ralph asked me to bring you a letter." Ralph was Vee's father, the one who'd also been unable to love again.

"How is he? You see much of him?" I asked her.

"He's really well. I don't see a lot of him, but he and Mom kept things civil and so he invited us to his wedding last month."

I accidentally spilled some of my wine down my mouth. "His wedding?"

Amelia leaped from the table, grabbed a napkin and dabbed at my mouth. She was too near, invading my personal space, and I took the napkin from her hand and jumped down from my stool, pretending to wash my mouth at the sink.

"Yeah. He met the most lovely woman. Her name's Belle. Anyway, we were chatting at the wedding and he said if I was coming to Manhattan, I should look you up. That he wondered if you were okay. You never kept in touch with any of us..." Her voice tapered off.

I chose not to reply.

"So, I came to the apartment. Your address was easy to Google, your privacy settings are lame, dude, and I met Mary, who is lovely by the way, and I may have thought you'd remarried an older woman, but she set me straight and said I was welcome to take a guest room for the night. She said I was just what you needed." She shrugged.

"Mary thinks I live in the past a little too much." I explained.

"Well, I need showing around Manhattan and I kind of threw caution to the wind and came here with only one job lead." She took a large gulp of wine.

"Okay, okay. This is all a little much to take in." I told her. "How about you stay here this week? I have plenty of room. You can do whatever business you need to do, and I can get caught up with what's happening with your family. Maybe I shouldn't have completely lost touch, but at the time it seemed the easiest thing to do."

"I still miss her." Said Amelia. Her stare made me feel uncomfortable, like she was trying to read my mind, assess how I felt about her sister after all these years.

I nodded. "We'll talk about your sister. But not now, okay?"

She nodded back.

"Right now, I need to work on some emails, so how about you go get used to your room or you can chill in the living room and I'll see you in the morning at breakfast?"

"Sounds great. Can I take the rest of the bottle of wine?" She looked at me with a begging expression on her face. It reminded me of what I saw at the club and I quickly turned away.

"Sure."

"Cool. See you tomorrow." She said breezily. Then she kissed my cheek and skipped out of the room.

I opened a second bottle of wine, filled up my glass and went into the study; Ralph's letter tucked under my armpit. Once in the privacy of my own space, I placed my wine glass and the letter down on my desk and slumped in my chair.

Amelia was like a hurricane and I felt unbalanced like someone clutching a tree branch, holding on for dear life.

In one night, my past had come hurtling back into my future, threatening my safety and my sanity.

I refused to think about Amelia herself, about how she looked. I shook my head as if I could shake the thoughts right out of my mind, but they kept repeating.

If she was at the club, you'd have wanted her.

She smelled beautiful.

She was full of life.

She lit up the apartment.

Then I reminded myself I was dead inside and she was my dead wife's half-sister, and I reached for Ralph's letter.

Son,
   It's been a while, I know. I wanted to get in touch and I picked up the phone many times, but I couldn't do it. I figured you had your reasons for cutting yourself

off from everyone and I knew how you felt. I did the same when Connie left me. So why now? I hear you say. Well, Henry, I met a woman. Despite telling you I'd never love again. Belle just came into my life— my new accountant could you believe it? And, well, it hit me like a ton of bricks, son. I actually think I love Belle more than I ever loved Connie. Now, steady on. I don't want ya spluttering that you'll never meet anyone you'll love more than you did my daughter. It might be that time has dulled my feelings and that my love for both was huge. All I'm saying is I found the capacity to love again. Yes, Connie wasn't cruelly taken away from me like my daughter/your wife was, but still, I wanted to let you know, your heart still does have the capacity for love inside. I know it because it's happened to me. Belle is younger than me and we're having a baby. My new baby will never be Vee, but maybe she'll go some way to fill the void left when my daughter departed the earth, the void of looking to the future and thinking of grandchildren and old age. Hell, I thought I'd be cuddling grandkids now, not about to start again myself at the age of 55!

I've kept tabs on you Henry. I know about your club and I know there's been no one serious in your life. So, I'm reaching out to you. Life is short. You don't have to seek love, but why not give it a chance to come find you? Be more open to dating instead of spending all your time in that club with people who don't give a damn. My address is enclosed, and any time you feel like popping over to see me, to meet my new wife (and my new daughter when she appears)-well, son, you are more than welcome.

Now I know this letter has been delivered to you by Amelia. If there's any work-related stuff—not the club jeez—you can get her involved in, her mom would be forever in your debt. Due to what happened with Vee, well, let's just say, Amelia's had an overprotected and sheltered existence, and Connie's scared she's going to settle over there and go wild. That she's going to lose her too.

I'm signing off now, my hand is hurting. People don't tend to write letters these days, do they? Just think about things and live a little. You didn't die that day, Henry. Vee did. Would she want you to have mourned for her for all this time?

Ralph.

With trembling hands, I placed the letter on the side and moved to my bedroom with my wine glass. I collected the bottle on the way past the kitchen and I drank myself into a stupor as the words from his letter circled the drain of my mind.

CHAPTER THREE

Amelia

Holy fuck. What was I doing here? I sat back against the headboard of the guest room bed, wine in hand. I'd told Henry I'd come to his home to deliver Ralph's letter and while that wasn't an outright lie, it wasn't the entire reason I was here either.

My imagination had led me here. Faded and scant memories of a man who had loved my sister. Someone I'd remembered as a prince. He could tell me things about Vee that I didn't know, that I'd been too young to know. I could make the vision of the person in my mind a reality. I had been just nine years old when I'd lost my sister. Far too young to experience such grief and so I found it had hit me again later in life. Times like when I got my period or had a crush on a guy at school. Times when it would be too embarrassing to talk to Mom, but an older sister who'd trodden the path before could have been a great adviser. Instead, it was like I barely knew her at all. She'd been fourteen years older than me and by the time I was properly aware of my big sister she'd moved away from home. She'd gotten along with Ralph okay, but the moment she could, she had left the family home. She had a brilliant mind Mom said and was a billionaire in property by the age of twenty-one. To me she was a hero, an enigma. I had family photos of us, photos with my big sister hugging me and smiling fondly at me. However, the real keeper of her secrets, of what she was like in personality, was held within the cold tomb of Henry Carter. That's how my mom had described him, anyway. She said he'd lost touch, had found it too difficult to remain around us. He'd thrown himself into his businesses—a club my parents thought I knew nothing about, and his property business. The business my sister had set up. She'd always said there would be a job for me when I was older and now I'd come to see if Henry would let me take that job. But if I was to get anywhere with him, I could see I was going to have to tread very carefully, go slowly. He was like a timid, but feral cat-wary and watching. As soon as I had sat across from him at the kitchen island, I could see I'd thrown his carefully ordered world upside down and that he was struggling to think straight. It was why I'd agreed I'd see him in the morning. Henry Carter needed to process things. He needed the time to consider his options. I had no idea what was in the letter my mom's first husband, Ralph-Vee's father-had sent him, but Ralph had asked me to make sure he was all right after reading it, so I would ask him about it in the morning.

I stared around the classic looking room with its high ceilings, high windows and muted tones of beiges and creams. It was beautiful and a much nicer room than anything I would be able to rent. When Henry had said I could stay the week I had breathed a huge sigh of relief. It had saved me asking him if I could stay.

Taking a drink of wine, I rested my head back and closed my eyes. My thoughts taking me back in time.

"What's it like being in love, Vee?" I asked my big sister. She was getting married soon. Her boyfriend, Henry, was like one of the princes in *my fairy tale books. He had longish blond hair, all floppy over his face and when he smiled, it was like his face was sunshine. He gave my sister the sunshine look all the time. "Is it like sunshine?" I added.*

Vee stroked my face.

"Sometimes. Well, a lot of the time, it's like sunshine. It makes you feel all happy and warm inside, you know?" I nodded avidly.

"But it's not like those fairy tales I keep catching you reading." My face dulled. "Sometimes we argue, just like anyone. That could be the thunder and lightning, I guess, and sometimes we can get upset with each other and I guess that's the rain? But then the sun comes back out and everything is lovely again."

"But is it mainly sunshine."

She nodded. "It's mainly sunshine, Lia." (She was the only person who ever called me that. I was her special Lia.)

I beamed at her words. "I thought so."

We didn't know that the lightning would strike her down and leave ongoing storm damage.

Death is strange when you're young. You don't fully understand what is happening. All I knew was my princess sister had died and her prince had left forever, brokenhearted.

For years I had kept all my family photos in my room. I poured over photographs of Vee and of Henry. Eventually, as my teens hit, I found myself looking more and more at the photos of Henry. The prince with the smiling face, and I wondered whether he'd found another princess, another wife. But I'd searched for him via the internet and realized pretty quickly that he'd never settled down again. He was broken, just like me. We were missing a piece. A piece called Vee. I needed to find him and talk to him.

When I'd walked into the room, those kid-like feelings of seeing Prince Henry had come to the fore. He was Mr. Sunshine and I'd flung my arms around him. Then he'd held me at arms-length and I'd seen in his eyes that there was no sun shining there anymore. His gaze was intense. His long, prince-like hair now short and stripped away like Delilah had done a Samson on him.

But he was beautiful. The man was a beautiful storm, and I'd realized the truth of why I was really there. I'd crushed on my prince for many long years while I had mourned my sister and now I'd found him. A broken prince I was determined to save.

To bring the sunshine back.

For a short while the next morning as the alarm on my cell phone slowly woke me, I wondered where I was. The vast king bed dwarfed my thin frame and the thick comforter was wrapped around my legs. I kicked it off and stared at the ceiling. It was my first full day in Manhattan. As I didn't know how I would be spending the day yet, I fixed my hair into a pony-tail, placed a robe over the top of my pajamas, and made my way toward the kitchen. The aroma of fresh coffee coupled with bacon drifted down the landing and my stomach growled in anticipation.

"Good morning, Amelia. Did you sleep well?" Mary turned away from the stove. "Take a seat and I'll bring you some breakfast. Coffee, and bacon and eggs, okay?"

"Oh my, that sounds like heaven, Mary. Thank you." I said honestly as my stomach growled with the thought of a home-cooked breakfast.

"Toast is on the table."

She brought my food over and I added some buttered toast and tucked in heartily. The food was delicious, and I told her so while still chewing.

"It's nice to see someone enjoying my food."

I turned to her and tilted my head. "Do you

mean Henry doesn't enjoy your food, or other, erm, people?"

"There are never other people." She emphasized the word other as she spoke it. "Henry always says thank you, but I never see the look on his face I just saw on yours."

"He's a mess, isn't he?" I asked her, even though I already knew the answer.

"He's a complex man. A hugely successful businessman. But he's closed off. Emotional situations shut him down. He avoids them."

I picked up my coffee, "How?"

Mary paused for a moment in thought. "Say an acquaintance of his is getting married. He'll send them the most perfect present he can get them. It will be carefully considered, but he'll always have a business trip that means he can't attend the occasion."

"Weddings are boring; sounds like a great excuse to get out of them." I quipped.

A small smile appeared on Mary's face. "Well, there is that. I've four daughters. I have to admit that by the fourth one's wedding, I was praying none of them remarry! It's more than that though. It's like he can't face anything like that. Still. After all this time."

Mary placed a hand over her chest. "I'm sorry, Amelia. I'm forgetting she was your sister."

I waved her off, "It's fine, Mary. I'm the opposite of Henry. I like to talk about my sister because I don't remember her all that much. We, as you know, had different parents and Vee was fourteen years older than me. She stayed over sometimes though, once she'd left, just to see me."

"It must have been very difficult for you."

"It was strange because my mom changed. She became very overprotective, which now I'm older I understand, but at the time it was hard. She wouldn't let me do the things other kids my age did. I couldn't rollerblade or ride a horse. I felt like Rapunzel, you know, stuck in my ivory tower."

"Morning."

Mary and I turned our heads toward the doorway simultaneously and there he was—Henry. Already immaculately dressed in a sharp gray suit, with a pale gray shirt, and a black and navy striped tie. He sat down at the kitchen island and Mary passed him a coffee and a slice of toast.

"Are you not having the lovely breakfast Mary's cooked for you?" I asked him.

He looked up at me, a frown on his face. "I only

ever have coffee and toast. I need to rush to the office."

"But she cooked, there's bacon and—"

"I cooked for you, Amelia. I wanted to make sure you got a good start to your day."

I blushed a little, surprised and heart-warmed. "Mary, you shouldn't have. Thank you."

"It was my pleasure—like I said before—to see someone enjoy my cooking."

"Cook Henry some bacon and eggs please." I asked.

"Amelia." Henry warned. "I'm in a rush."

"Are you? I thought you were the boss? Delegate, or be late. It's not every day you get a surprise visitor."

"I got a surprise visitor yesterday," he smirked. "Today, I know you're here."

"Well, I want to see you for a while. Who knows I may leave today and go get a job in Manhattan and not return, so you'd better hang around to see me right now." I stuck my tongue in my cheek.

Henry sighed. "Fine. Mary, could you please fix me some bacon and eggs, so I may breakfast with Amelia, and if you haven't eaten yourself yet, please fix some for yourself too, and let's all sit down and entertain Amelia while she's still here." He picked up his cell, "Ashley. Something's come up. Can you move my morning appointment to tomorrow? Thanks." He placed his cell back on the table. "Satisfied? The boss moved things, so you can watch him eat bacon."

I laughed, and Mary joined in. We both looked at the very serious looking Henry who sounded as if he'd just had a tantrum. Then Henry began laughing too.

"Actually, the aroma in here is so good, it's not a hardship to stay and eat a cooked breakfast. I'll have to hit the gym harder tonight, that's all."

"You go to the gym a lot?" I asked him.

"Most days. It's on the fifth floor. I'll get you a guest pass." He explained.

"Excellent. When will you be going?"

"I never have a set time, just when I get home from work."

"Well, let me know, and I'll come with you. You can show me the ropes."

He turned to me, "You do realize there are instructors there who can 'show you the ropes', and the equipment, and the weights?"

"Yeah, but I'm shy, so I'd rather go there with you."

Mary placed a plate of food in front of him and refilled his coffee.

"Help me, Mary. This girl has arrived and is causing chaos. She's only been here a few hours."

Mary took a seat at the table and smirked at me while Henry sliced up a piece of bacon.

"Yes, I've noticed the difference already," she said, and she winked at me.

CHAPTER FOUR

Henry

What was happening? I'd heard friendly chatter coming from the normally quiet kitchen. Usually in a morning, once she'd served me my coffee and toast, Mary left me to my laptop, cell or the morning news. But today, the kitchen seemed more, well, alive. I took in how happy Mary was when Amelia had thanked her for her breakfast and then there I was, forced to eat one myself.

And I had to admit, it was delicious.

Ashley, my main assistant, would have no doubt alerted my team that I'd been kidnapped or had had a mental breakdown by now as I never failed to show for a meeting, never rearranged anything.

When Amelia had said she might not stick around long, I had thrown caution to the wind. I didn't remember the last time I'd had a vacation. Maybe I could open a few windows in my schedule, so I could spend some time catching up on what had happened with Vee's family.

Amelia sat on a stool with her hair tied back, looking fresh-faced and comfortable, like she'd lived here her whole life, not arrived the evening before. With a guest robe from her bathroom wrapped over what appeared to be pajamas, she seemed in no rush to go anywhere or do anything.

"What are your plans for the day, Amelia?" I asked her.

"Well, I have an interview this afternoon."

"Really? Where?"

She tapped the side of her nose. "I'll tell you if I get it. So, this morning I'm trying to keep zen about the whole thing. If it's meant to be, I'll get it, right?" She accepted another cup of coffee from Mary. "And after that, I have no plans, so I'll probably come back here and annoy Mary while she fixes dinner."

"Anything in particular you'd like?" Mary asked her.

"Hey, you're mine, not hers." I laughed.

"Can we have steak and fries?" Amelia asked.

"Okay, listen to the girl." I said, "steak and fries and some of that gorgeous tasting re-fried beans thing you do, oh and salsa."

"You like my re-fried beans and the salsa?" Mary asked.

"It's wonderful."

"Mary didn't know you liked anything she cooked you. Did you never tell her?" said Amelia.

I noticed Mary hung her head low, no doubt embarrassed by Amelia's brashness.

I sat back and thought about it. "Do you know, probably not. I'm either home after Mary's left, which is ninety-five percent of the time, or I'm still thinking about work."

"Henry Carter, you're a jerk. Apologize to Mary immediately."

I got down off my stool and stood, head bowed, next to my red-faced housekeeper who was shaking her head at Amelia. I grabbed her hand. "Mary, I apologize wholeheartedly for my ignorance. Your food is amazing, and I especially love your re-fried beans and salsa. Would you do me the honor of preparing these tonight?"

"Oh God, I think I liked quiet H, better." Joked Mary.

"H?" Amelia asked.

"That's what everybody calls me." I told her.

"Why?"

I shrugged. "A nickname. To keep things professional."

"Well, I'm not calling you that. Your name's always been Henry to me." She said, and I saw tears threatening her eyes.

I placed down my cutlery.

"Mary, that was exquisite, but I really must leave now." I hopped off the stool. "Good luck with the interview, Amelia." I shouted back into the room.

I drove to the office cursing. I was letting this girl, this woman, get to me. Why? Because of her connection to my past? She was already changing things, blurring the lines. My god, I'd breakfasted with my housekeeper this morning. The traffic lights changed to red, and I drummed my fingers against the steering wheel. Amelia was already starting to bring Henry back, but hadn't he left a long time ago, along with his wife?

Having driven to the headquarters of Carter Property Enterprises, I threw my keys at the valet and headed up to the twenty-third floor. Situated a floor below Club S, it was easy to keep an eye on both businesses from here. Only a privileged few knew what happened on the floor above.

"What's my schedule, Ashley?" I asked as I walked in. She picked up her iPad and rushed into the office after me.

"Macy's bringing your coffee, Mr. Carter, as I wasn't sure what time you'd be in."

"That's fine. Now remind me of what fun is in store today. Please tell me I'm buying property. I'm in a spending mood."

Ashley looked at me warily, and I realized I'd probably never joked around with her before in the slightest. In fact, I would never have asked her about my schedule because I always knew exactly what I was doing from day to day. I was going to find a four o'clock appointment booked with a shrink if I didn't explain myself.

"I have family over. Kinda family anyway. It's caused some disruption to my usual schedule."

"Right." There was no mistaking the relief on Ashley's face that I wasn't having a breakdown.

"Well, you are seeing Aidan at eleven and then from one pm it's the interviews for your deputy position."

"That's today? Shoot. Let me see the files as soon as possible please."

"Yes, Sir. Anything else?"

"Yeah. Can you arrange for a selection of donuts

to be here along with a good strong coffee for when Mr. Hall arrives? He has a sweet tooth."

"Already done, Mr. Carter."

"Thank you, Ashley." I told her, wondering now if I'd ever thanked her for what she did either. "I'm very grateful for everything you do to keep me in order. Get yourself a coffee and donut too, okay?"

"Yes, Sir."

"And please call me H when there's no one else around, just Mr. Carter in front of other people in a professional capacity."

"Yes, Sir, I mean, H." She rushed from the room.

I sat back and let out a hearty laugh. I had to admit that watching the bemused faces of my staff as I acted a little human around them was kind of entertaining. Then I realized that up until now I must have seemed like some kind of robot and suddenly it wasn't as funny as before.

I searched through the three applications of the interviewees. They all had merit. All three had no identifiable information, so that there was no bias before the interviews. I had asked Aidan to sit in on the interviews along with Katy, a member of my human resources department so that I had an extra business opinion. Ultimately, if this person was going to be my second-in-command, I'd need to be able to trust them and also get along with them, albeit on a professional level.

I walked into the interview room with Aidan and Katy and the first two interviews went fine although a gut feeling told me neither was suitable. As a businessman, gut feeling went a long way, you seemed to develop an inbuilt suspicion of people. "Okay," said Katy, "I'll go and fetch Lia."

And then there she was in front of me, wearing a navy suit and looking the height of professionalism. Her blonde hair tied up in a bun, Amelia had on a white blouse, simple jewelry and carried herself with confidence. She walked over and shook all three of our hands and thanked us for interviewing her before she took her seat. The only hint at nerves came from her taking a sip of water from the glass placed in front of her by Aidan.

I looked over her application again. She'd worked for an estate agents for the last few years, selling exclusive properties in The Hamptons. She'd taken a business degree at University. Clever girl. I had severely underestimated Amelia, imagining her to be the spoiled daughter of overprotective parents.

Her interview was flawless and then she was asked to leave and that we would let her know our decision later that day.

I told Katy I'd be in touch, and Aidan followed me back to my office where I poured us both a scotch before I sat behind my desk.

"Well," Aidan loosened his tie. "I know which one I'd be choosing, though I'd be distracted wondering what she looked like with that hair swinging while she sucked my dick."

"Amelia is Vee's younger sister. Well, half-sister." I told him.

His jaw dropped. Aidan was rarely speechless, but this time it took him a good couple minutes before he found his voice again.

"Holy fucking shit. Did you know?"

I sighed. "Not one clue and she arrived at my house last night. Mary put her in the spare room. I had breakfast with her this morning. She asked if I'd take some time to show her around Manhattan this week. Said she'd come to look for a job and mentioned she had an interview this afternoon. Failed to mention it was for my company."

"Sly. I like it." He said.

"You keep away from Amelia." I shot back.

He held his hands up in surrender. "Dude. Heard loud and clear. How old is she anyway?"

I sat and thought about it. "Twenty-three, I think. She was nine when Vee passed."

"Well, H. Wake the fuck up, man. She's going to be dating or doing dirty stuff with men by this age so maybe you can cut me some slack and maybe let me take your sister-in-law out one night, for just dinner of course."

For some reason my neck stiffened. I didn't want to imagine Amelia like that. Like how Aidan and I viewed the women at the club. Of course, at twenty-three she wouldn't be the innocent I seemed to picture her as.

"No. At least not right now. Let her get settled. So, what do you think? Do I give her the job?"

"You'd be a fool not to. She has all the right qualifications and you know her. You know you can trust her?"

I nodded. "I think so."

"Then that goes a hell of a long way. You need someone assisting as soon as possible unless you're finally going to see sense and hand that club over to me."

I gave him a wry look.

"Can't fault a man for trying, and I'm going to keep trying." Aidan sat back, his hands behind his head. "I want to be the King of the sex world. I want clubs. There's my movie business now. I'm setting up my publishing company for books like Fifty Shades, capitalizing on Mummy Porn. Going to make movies for women. I'd have a women's fantasy night at the club."

"You have it all worked out." I smiled.

"Yeah, I just need the club." He whined.

"Maybe soon, Aidan. Just leave it with me. I have a lot to think about."

"Seriously?" Once again Aidan looked speechless. "I didn't honestly think you'd ever give up that club."

"Me neither, but I'm having some kind of midlife crisis this week. Pondering the meaning of life and what I want to do with the rest of it. I'm wondering if Amelia's been sent as some kind of sign from the universe that I need to get my shit together."

I noticed Aidan bit his lip.

"Out with it. What are you wanting to say?"

He cleared his throat. "Look, man, I never had a wife. Had a couple serious relationships but never took them anywhere near that level. I cannot imagine what it must have been like to lose someone you love that suddenly."

I looked at my desk, the paperwork had become more interesting.

"I know we don't speak like this, but H, I'm in agreement with fate here and I don't even admit to believing in that shit, but if you have a second-in-command, you should have more time available to you once she's trained, to either take the business further or to take more of a backseat, and if she's hanging around for a while, it's a bit of company rather than you sitting in that apartment all on your lonesome all the time."

I nodded.

"Does she know about the club?"

"No. Let's keep it that way for now."

Aidan sighed. "Do you think that's a good idea? Someone is bound to mention it to her."

I sat for a while with my chin in my hand while I thought things through. "I'll tell her this week. We need to get to know each other better, and I need to explain the property side of the business to her. But the club side can wait. For a few days at least."

"Okay, man. You're the boss."

"Thanks for sitting in with me, Aidan. As it turned out I didn't need the extra opinion, but I appreciate it just the same."

"Anytime. Will you be at the club later?"

"No. I'm going to keep it on the down low the next couple days. Until I get Amelia settled in. Now she has a job she might want to get her own place. I'll see if there's anything I have that could be suitable.

Then I promised to show her around Manhattan. It's going to be a busy few days."

"Well, I'll keep an eye on my potential future business for you." He winked.

"Go for it. Organize that women's night if you want."

"Not a chance. Not until that baby is in my name."

I laughed.

"Right. Thanks for the drink." Aidan got to his feet, reached over and shook my hand. "You try to relax a little over the next few days and why not take note of the fact you have an attractive young blonde to spend time with? Things are looking up, bro."

"She's my wife's younger sister."

"Half-sister, right? And looking isn't a crime. Hell, not looking at her is a crime."

"Okay, you've outstayed your welcome. Out you go."

"Gorgeous breasts," he mouthed in the doorway, while miming running his hands over them. As the door closed behind him, I gulped down the rest of my scotch and poured another.

Too much was happening. My brain felt like it was on a spin cycle, and I needed an hour or so to get my head together. However, I also needed to call

Katy to let her know Amelia was our choice, and then I had back-to-back meetings all afternoon.

Like I'd done with so much of my life, I had to shut my thoughts down and hide them inside of me for another time.

W hen my working day was over, I felt like hitting the gym. But first, I needed to head home for steak, fries, re-fried beans, and salsa.

I was pleased to find Amelia seated in the kitchen. I hated the formality of the dining room and rarely ever used it. Amelia was still dressed in her interview clothes, her hair still up.

"Miss Porter."

"Sorry about that, Henry. I didn't know how to play it, but I wanted to be interviewed and accepted on my own merits, hence I put a different surname on my application and called myself Lia."

"Yes, when you're expecting a Lia Porter, it's a bit of a shock when Amelia Wilson walks in for an interview."

She smiled, a wide, face engulfing smile. She didn't give a damn. "Your face." Then she laughed, heartily.

She hopped off her stool and added steaks to the pan.

"That's Mary's job." I told her.

"Mary did everything else. These needed cooking fresh. I wasn't making her stay to do that when I'm perfectly capable of cooking them myself."

I looked through some post while she cooked. She put a plate of food in front of me. I stood and got some water for the table.

"No wine tonight?" She asked.

"I'll be going to the gym later."

"Oh yes, I remember now. I'll come too."

I started to feel annoyed. It was only her second day here and now Amelia was in my apartment, at my place of work, and now she wanted to accompany me to the gym. It was like a noose tightening around my neck. I needed space.

"So, can I now ask you the interview questions I wanted to ask but human resources would never have let me?" I stated.

"Sure." Amelia started to cut her steak.

"Question number one. Why do you want to work in property and work for me?"

Amelia finished chewing and swallowing the food in her mouth and then she placed her fork down.

"My sister loved property, and she loved you. I didn't know what to do with my life. I had/have no real interest in a career to be truthful. I did my business degree and then decided to try working with property. To see if I could discover what Vee had found so amazing. I enjoyed working at the realtor's, but I wouldn't say it was a passion. I don't think I've ever had one of those. So, I decided I'd come and work where she worked, for the company she founded. I've followed you on the internet for years. I saw the job advert. Decided it was like fate. I was meant to come here. I'll be brilliant at it. You won't regret hiring me."

"But you don't love it. Property?"

"Well that's yet to be seen because I've not worked for you before, but I've never been all consumed by a career before, no."

"So why do you think that is? Maybe you should pick out your own career rather than trying to follow your sister's footsteps." I snapped, irritated by her answers.

"Are you angry I've copied her, Henry?"

"I know you're not Vee."

"Ouch. I've certainly been made aware of that many times in my life, H. Thanks very much for the reminder."

She called me H, no doubt an insult to the years post-Vee. She hopped down off the stool. As she walked past me, I grabbed her shoulder.

"I didn't mean it like that, Amelia. What I meant was, what is the point of trying to see if you like the career path Vee liked? Why not do what you want to do? You must have a passion of your own."

"Yes. I want to be a mom. I want to have babies. That's my passion."

I flinched.

"But you kind of need a man in your life for families, and I've only ever met complete jerks." She stared me directly in the eyes. "I know you're not ready to talk about Vee, Henry. But I'm trying to gain some closure on what happened to my sister. I'm sick of living under a dark cloud about it all. I'm not dead. Everyone wants me to live half a life. I'm going to give this job my utter attention and professionalism. I owe it to my sister to carry on her dream, just like you've been doing. No more holding that burden all on your own, Henry. I'm here whether you like it or not."

"Please sit back down, Amelia, and finish your meal."

She reversed and sat back on her stool. "I don't know how long I'll stay in the post, but I'll make a difference while I'm there, and I'll stay to fully train someone else if I leave."

"You start tomorrow. There'll be no cooked breakfast. You'll meet me in my office at eight am sharp. I won't go lightly on you because you're family. You've a job to do. I need an assistant. I'm too busy. There'll be early starts and late finishes. I'm a workaholic. It's what's kept me going over the years. I kept the property business going as it was what Vee and I developed together. But I'm considering my future and whether I'm staying in business. So we turn up, do our best work, then go home and take one day at a time. If there's one thing I learned from what happened with Vee, there's no guarantee of the future, so I live in the moment."

"Don't you want to remarry, Henry? Have a family someday?"

"And risk it happening all over again?"

"The chances of a future wife having a brain tumor must be the same as those of a lottery win, surely?"

"Leave it, Amelia."

"Don't you want children?" She repeated.

"Yes, I wanted children." I finally exploded. "But when you lose a son in the womb, along with your wife, that kind of fucks things up a little. It's better to be who I am. Dead inside. I can't get hurt again that way."

"Wh-what do you mean, Henry? When did you lose a child?"

I looked at Amelia in horror. Her face was pale and her lips trembled.

I lowered my voice and spoke gently. "Vee was pregnant. Surely you knew that? She was four and a half months along."

Amelia shook her head. "I don't remember that, Henry. Did she tell me that? Did I know? Have I blocked it out?"

I shook my head. "I can't answer that. I don't know."

"She would have told me she was having a baby, wouldn't she? I'd have been so excited to get a baby niece or nephew. There has to be some explanation. There has to be." She let out a squeal of anguish. "You lost your wife and a son. Your future. I'm so sorry, Henry. So, so sorry."

I got down from my stool and wrapped my arms around her as she cried on my shoulder. She cried for me and what I'd lost as well as for the confusion she'd grown up with.

At that point I wished she'd never come here, but I held on to her just the same until she stopped.

Then I backed away from her.

"I'm not going to the gym, Amelia. I'm going to head off to a bar for an hour. It's been a bit heavy. Why don't you go lie down in your room and we'll talk some more tomorrow? I'll see you in the office at eight."

"Okay." She sniffed and left the room.

I changed my shirt, which was wet from her tears, and I drove to the club.

At the bar I downed three scotches in quick succession, and then I looked in all the rooms. I found one where a woman was in the room alone wearing a mask. Her bracelet was black with silver stars meaning she wanted to play. I guessed someone had just left her. She was lying on the bed, her legs open while her own hand strummed her clit. I went over to the bed and took over. I played with her pussy until she was on the brink of orgasm and then I turned her over onto all fours and I plunged my cock deep inside her. She groaned, whether with passion or faking it, I didn't give a damn. I thrust into her, pent up rage making me rough. I pinched her nipples hard with one hand while my other fisted in her hair, holding her in place as I thrust into her again and again until she climaxed around my cock. I turned her over again to face me and pulled her mask up until her mouth was uncovered and then I jerked off until my hot sticky cum spurted and hit her mouth and chin. I didn't stay to help her clean up. I felt both satisfied and unsatisfied as I moved away from the bed. I cleaned myself up and went back to the bar.

Sometimes I felt it was so much easier for those who died than those left behind. My oblivion was short lived. Alcohol wore off.

CHAPTER FIVE

Amelia

The night was a long one with little sleep. I was frustrated as I needed to call my mom to get answers to the new questions in my mind. Why would my sister not have told me she was having a baby? Perhaps she'd thought I was too young and was waiting until she showed more? That was probably it. I was being stupid. Things with Henry tonight had become heated and emotional. He'd left the apartment, slamming the door behind him, and I wondered if he'd gone to his club.

I also wondered if he'd tell me tomorrow about his other business when I was being shown around?

One thing was for sure. I was going to be a model employee.

Yes, I knew my being here was upsetting to Henry, and maybe bringing back memories he didn't want to face, but I couldn't apologize for what I was doing. I needed to do this to get my own life on track. For once, I was putting my own needs first. I'd enjoyed him comforting me when I'd cried and then I'd felt guilty. It was his loss, yet I was the one crying and being comforted? How did someone cope with the loss of their wife and child? Their whole future world. Well, he hadn't, had he? He'd buried it as deep as he'd buried his wife. If there was one goal I had for him while I was here, it was to get him to see life was worth taking chances for.

Eventually, in the early hours of the morning, I heard the door open and Henry stumbling down the corridor. Footsteps came all the way down to my room. The door pushed open slightly, and I quickly closed my eyes and let my mouth hang open, pretending to be asleep.

"What the fuck are you doing to me, Amelia." He whispered from the doorway.

Then I heard the door close and his footsteps stumbling back to his own room.

· · ·

He was gone, already at work when I went to the kitchen the next morning.

"Morning, Mary. I need all the coffee in the world today." I smiled at her.

"Are you excited about your first day?" She asked.

"Nervous." I replied honestly. "I know I can do the job, but with Henry knowing me, I don't want people thinking he's making allowances, or I got the job from being kind of family."

"How close were you to him, back then?" She asked me. I could tell Mary was fond of Henry and had developed a motherly relationship with him.

"I didn't really know him at all." I told her truthfully. "They eloped to get married, so I didn't get to be a bridesmaid or anything. Then they lived in Manhattan. He'd just bought them a house in The Hamptons, was bringing her home, when she passed. Then he went back to Manhattan and cut himself off from us all."

"You like him, don't you?" She asked me.

I hesitated, but only for a moment. It was a chance to admit how I felt for once. To get things off my chest.

"He was always like some mysterious Prince

Charming to me, Mary. I thought I'd built him up in my mind as a kind of fantasy, you know? But when I saw him, well, he's still like that to me. The unattainable prince. He was married to my sister. He's an impossibility, and maybe that makes him even more attractive? I have intimacy issues, so pursuing someone I'll never have is typical Amelia territory."

"Well, I have no idea if he is, or will ever be, attracted to you, or whether you'll forever be Vee's little sister, but I do know this. I've seen more life in him the last two days than I've seen in all the years I've worked for him. I've seen Henry. Your being here is good for him. So I hope you stay. Just be gentle with him."

"I will. If nothing else, I'm sure we'll be friends."

"Would you like some bacon? I know H said to hurry and get to work."

"Can I have a bacon sandwich to go?" I hopped off my stool. "I'd better go and get ready."

I arrived at work with ten minutes to spare, and one of his assistants asked me to wait outside his office. At eight am sharp his office door opened, and he looked out with an annoyed look on his face before spotting me. He gestured me inside his office.

"You thought I'd be late, didn't you?" I smirked.

"I know how much you love Mary's breakfasts, and I didn't think you'd be able to resist."

It was straight into business mode after that. Henry himself showed me around the building and introduced me to people. I was assigned an assistant, Jessica, and already had a diary full of appointments. Some were more introductions to people, such as Tyler, from IT, who gave me an induction to the computer systems, etc, and set me up with pass-words. At other times I had meetings to attend with Henry himself. I was kept busy and went home to the apartment every night exhausted. Henry wasn't around and so I spent most evenings in the living room, curled up watching TV while I processed the day.

Henry had a last minute 'business trip' at the weekend which took him away from the apartment. I started to wonder if he was avoiding me. I'd barely seen him apart from spending time in meet-ings with him. My following week's diary was pretty much the same. I was learning the ropes. He'd not mentioned the club. Once I knew he was not going to be around at the weekend, I called up some girlfriends and had them show me Manhattan at night.

By the time Monday came around again, I was frustrated with Henry's apparent avoidance of me.

As I sat at my computer on Monday, studying some very exciting company policies, Jessica buzzed through.

"Do you have time to see Aidan Hall? He's a business partner of Mr. Carter's. Mr. Carter is not in, so he was wondering if he could see you instead?"

"I know Aidan. Yes, send him in." I told her.

I got up from my seat as Aiden walked through the door.

Aiden Hall was a very attractive man. At around six feet tall, he was dark haired and dark eyed. He had a friendly look on his face, though I could tell by looking at him that if he wanted to, I'd bet he could put a brooding, chill factor on people.

"Hey, Amelia. I thought I'd see how you were settling in. What's that look on your face? Do I have pen on my lip or something?" He felt at his face. It was a hint of vulnerability and it made me chuckle.

"I was just wondering what your deal making face looks like. You know, when you're trying to close in on an important deal and you're being fucked over. What does your intimidating stare look like?"

"Ah, I don't have one. I just charm everyone and they fall at my feet." He laughed.

I shook my head at him. "Coffee?"

"Yes please." He sat across from me while I asked Jessica for two coffees.

"So how are you settling in?" He asked me again.

"Busy." I told him, "although this morning I had some free time, hence I decided to read up on some exciting company policies."

"I'm glad I came in to save you from that then."

"So what did you want Henry for? Anything I can help you with?" I relaxed back in my chair. I liked Aidan even though I didn't know him well. There was something about him, maybe his easy-going manner, which put me at ease.

"Ah, I knew H wasn't around this morning. I just came to check in on you and that was my excuse."

"Right."

"So, how was your first week?"

A knock came at the door.

"Come in."

Jessica brought in both our coffees.

"White, two sugars?" She asked Aidan. He was obviously a regular fixture around here. After she left, I tried to take a sip of my too hot coffee.

"So, how do you know Henry then? What business do you do with him? I see you're on my schedule to meet anyway, Thursday at four."

"That's why I'm here. I wondered if you'd like to go to dinner instead? Far nicer to discuss business over great food than sit in my boring office."

I crossed one leg over the other and looked at him shrewdly. "Is there an agenda to this dinner?"

"No agenda, just like I said, nicer surroundings." He changed his posture, sitting open-legged with his arms resting on his knees and hands between his thighs, fingers intertwined. He looked up at me, gaze direct. "So how about it?"

"Fine. I like Italian." I told him.

"And that's my business game face," he told me laughing. "See how effective it is?"

I guffawed. "Well played, Aidan, well played. I didn't even know you were gaming me."

"See, mostly you win business with honesty and charm. I'm not much of a player and can't do aloof to save my life. Now, I'm no pushover. I'm very, very ambitious, but I can't manage H's icy, brooding stare that makes people wilt under the pressure, so I go with being the good guy."

"And are you a good guy?" I asked, an eyebrow raised.

"Mostly." He answered.

"So you met Henry through business then?"

62

He took a fraction too long to answer and so I made a calculated guess.

"His other business, right? The Club?"

"You know about the club?" He asked, his voice slower, like he was treading carefully.

"Of course."

Aidan visibly relaxed. "Oh thank fuck, he told you. I thought I was going to have to pretend forever that there wasn't a sex club on the floor above us."

I flinched and was pleased he'd been distracted by lifting up his coffee cup.

"Yes, well I felt if I was his second-in-command I should know everything." I lied. "He was cagey in telling me how you knew him though." I tried to lead Aidan on.

"Well, that's his story to tell, not mine. But I reckon he's getting bored with the club and I'm happy to take it off his hands, so put in a good word for me, won't you?"

"You want to buy a sex club?"

"Yes, it will go nicely alongside my new movie studio and publishing company."

"You own a movie company?"

"Yes, it makes adult movies. GoDown Films. I acquired it recently. The Club would make a fabulous backdrop for a series of movies and could become an extension of the movies, a kind of, experience it for yourself." He closed his mouth and chewed his lip. "Why, Amelia, you have a way of getting people to divulge private information. I just gave away my business plan to you."

"I can keep a secret." I told him.

"Can you?" He said. "Then don't tell Henry we switched the office for dinner until after we've eaten. He'll think I have ulterior motives."

"Well, if you did, what concern is it of Henry's?" I asked, my curiosity peaked. Had Henry warned him off?

"I like my balls where they are, rather than strung up somewhere. Once we've had dinner, and he realizes you're still intact, he might relax a little."

At his comment my face burned with an intensity that meant I thought I was going to need dousing in water.

"Are you okay?" Aidan asked. "What did I say to embarrass you? I'm so sorry, Amelia, it wasn't my intention."

I could see the cogs whirring in that business mind as he recounted the conversation.

"Oh. Jesus."

"Aidan, please."

"How old are you? You're like twenty-four

aren't you?"

"Twenty-three."

"Then how the fuck?"

I held a finger up to my mouth for him to quieten down.

"How am I intact? How am I still a virgin at the age of twenty-three? Because I'm frigid." Now my face burned even more. "I get so far and then I just, well, haven't been able to get any further." I sit back. "I cannot believe I am having this conversation with you. Please don't tell a soul, and especially not Henry."

"Amelia. I wouldn't say a word. Have you been to see someone about this though? There must be professionals who can help you?"

I shook my head. "No. I truly believe I just haven't met the right guy. I've never met anyone I've felt relaxed with, anyone who I honestly wanted to sleep with, and I think it's my body's way of telling me they aren't right for me."

"Why not go up to the club one night?" Aidan suggested. "Just go to watch and see if anything you see especially turns you on. Maybe you're attracted to women, or threesomes. You can just observe there."

"I don't know how the club works." I told him

honestly.

"I'll take you Thursday, after dinner."

I started to protest.

"Not to do anything, Amelia. Though I'm not going to lie and say I don't find you attractive because I do, but there's no way I would make moves on you. Not with my relationship with H. If things developed between us over time, then that's something else, but right now, you're my new business buddy and it won't be the first time I've taken a colleague to Club S to show them the ropes." He winked.

I could imagine it. All boys together. In their element at some bawdy sex show.

"Okay. I'm intrigued. So after dinner, I'd like to see what happens there."

"Amelia?"

"Yes."

"How did you know about the club, really? H didn't tell you, did he? You don't know enough."

"Ah, found out."

"You don't know enough. H would have given you extensive information as his new second-in-command. So, spill the beans."

"I read the rumors about the place on the net."

"Fuck. I guess I've yet to work out your game

face 'cause I just got played."

"Feminine wiles. If you've got them, why not use them?" I laughed.

"So, no talk of dinner and no talk of the club with H, or I won't take you." He gave me a cold, hard stare.

I started laughing again. "So that's your attempt at a Henry Carter business face I take it?"

He laughed again, himself. "Now you see why I stick to what I know. So, how about on Thursday, we meet at my office at four as planned? I'll show you around as I'm supposed to, and then I'll drive you back to yours to get changed."

He caught my frown.

"H is away at a conference Thursday evening. I will wait outside for you if you'd rather."

I made a note that I needed to study Henry's whereabouts more closely. I was supposed to be his deputy, and although I was still in training at the moment I should still know where he was.

"Then we'll go for the Italian, and then I'll take you to the club. So dress in something black, maybe with silver."

"Oh, yes?"

"It's kinda a theme. You'll see." He told me.

He finished the rest of his coffee and then got to

his feet. "Well, I'd better go slay. Can't be chatting all day long. That doesn't assist with my billion-dollar empire."

I rolled my eyes.

He pointed at me. "Deletes 'impressed by wealth' off my list. I can see I need to try harder." He winked and walked over to me, holding out his hand. I shook it.

"You'd need to try much harder than that." I told him. "If you were trying to impress me as a date. Which I am not. I'm a colleague."

Aidan held a hand to his heart. "Ouch, straight to the chest. You know how to bring a guy down. You'll do well in this post." He smiled. "You don't take any bullshit."

"Can smell it a mile off." I told him. "Now, go make more billions and leave me to study health and safety." I made a mock yawn.

"See you Thursday." He said, before heading out of the door.

"See you then," I replied. As he left, I sat back a moment and smiled. I could do worse than to see how a non-date with Aidan Hall went. Maybe it would take my mind off the brooding, unattainable Mr. Carter.

Maybe... maybe not.

CHAPTER SIX

Aidan

I really liked Amelia, but I had a feeling her heart belonged somewhere else. From what I knew of my friend, H, she was wasting her time. Or maybe not. I decided to have a little fun and call H on his cell.

"Carter."

"Yeah. Just thought I'd let you know I checked in on your deputy this morning and she was very well-behaved."

There was a silence and then H's icy, do-not-fuck-with-me tone came down the line. "Care to elaborate?"

"She was reading company policy. Who does that, H? You have spare time, so you read company policy, not browse the Internet, or eat a sneaky chocolate cupcake."

"She's determined to prove that I was right to hire her."

"You sure about that? Or is she wanting to impress you? Ever think she might have got the job to be closer to you?" I knew I was pushing him,, but I needed some clues.

"It's not like that."

"I really like her. I wouldn't seduce her because it could fuck up business, but I might ask her out sometime."

When H's voice came back, it sounded strangulated. "Well, give her some time to settle first. I don't want her scared away."

"But you wouldn't mind?" Push. Push. Push.

"It's not my place to mind. It's her life." There was a pause. "But if you hurt, her I will kill you."

No laughter followed his sentence. Just pure intent.

H had feelings for this woman though whether they were attraction or just fondness for someone from his past was yet to be discovered. But discover it I would. I would like nothing better than for my friend to find happiness, but if he wasn't interested, then I'd go for Amelia myself.

I couldn't wait for Thursday.

Manipulation and game playing was my specialty.

Amelia arrived at the office at three forty-five. My prior meeting had finished and so my assistant let her straight through.

"I did not realize you worked out of your house." She told me.

"Saves on renting office space." I shrugged. "Plus there's only me, and I was rocking around this enormous place on my own. Figured two birds, one stone." I got up from my seat, "let me show you around."

"You seriously want to show me your home? Like is it going to include a tour of the bedroom too?" She rolled her eyes in that endearing way she had.

"No, Amelia. Not even if you beg. Just the business floor for you." I smiled at her and she laughed in return.

I walked her around, describing how the interior had been changed so that all the living accommodation including the kitchen was on the second floor, and that the first floor had been altered to accommodate an office for myself, a general room with shared desk space for anyone who needed it, and a couple of meeting rooms, plus a reception.

"I love it. It makes perfect sense with your businesses being in different areas." She told me after she'd looked around. "So, if I need to escape from Henry, there's a desk here I can use?" She queried, while looking at the hot-desk area.

"Anytime. Why, do you think you'll need to escape from Henry?"

She sighed. "He seems to be avoiding me. Or maybe I'm paranoid, and he just really is that busy. He'd said he'd show me around Manhattan, but I guess that was before I became his employee. I suppose it would appear a little strange to people, if they saw us out together. I'm being stupid. That will be why he's avoiding me." She shrugged. "So perhaps if I come and work here occasionally, it'll give him a break. That, and it's probably time for me to look for someplace else to live."

"Have you tried asking him if there's a problem?"

"No. I've not had the opportunity, or it has felt awkward. When I first came here, we got on really well, but now it's like there's a problem. I know I need to ask him about it, but I'm hesitant. What if he sacks me or something?"

"He is not going to sack you. And if you need

someplace else to live in the meantime, you can always stay here. I have spare rooms galore in my home."

"Why have you bought a home far too large for you, Aidan?"

"The address and the prestige. Park Avenue looks very nice on my business cards."

"I shouldn't imagine the people who live around here would be very pleased about your association with making adult entertainment."

"You'd be surprised." I told her, and the tiniest blush caught her cheeks.

"Oh, Amelia. You need to get that embarrassment under control if we're going to visit Club S."

"Can't I wear a mask, or disguise?" She retorted.

"Only on Friday nights." I told her.

"God, I feel so naive." She said, her foot kicking against the edge of a desk.

"Amelia, you're like a breath of fresh air in Manhattan, lovely lady. Don't be embarrassed." I swiftly changed the subject. "Italian still?"

After dropping her home to get changed, we headed to the restaurant where I'd (well actually my assistant had being truthful), made reservations. We chattered amiably over dinner and I learned more about her upbringing as she learned more about the business. I told her little of my own past as to be honest, I didn't think she was all that interested. Her hunger for information on H shone through, and I would have had to be blind to not see the crush she had on him. Eventually, after several glasses of wine she admitted to it.

"It was a silly infatuation, like you get with a pop star. He was like some kind of mystery Prince Charming who had whisked my sister off her feet. Hey," she added, alcohol loosening her tongue. "How much do you know about Henry, about when my sister died?"

"I know he lost a child, too." I told her, "if that's what you are hinting at."

"I didn't know that." She admitted. Her eyes widened, and she looked very young and vulnerable. In that moment I imagined what the young Amelia, nursing a crush for her prince, would have looked like. "I found out last week." She confessed. "I had to call my mom to ask her why I'd never been told."

"And what did your mom say?"

Amelia began to tear up. "I'd better not say."

"Amelia." I placed a hand on hers. "I'm here if you want to talk, and I won't betray your secrets."

She took a deep breath.

"My mom told me that neither her nor Vee's

father had known she was pregnant. She'd not told anyone but Henry. But she let Henry believe that they knew."

"Why would she do that? It makes no sense."

"Because she wasn't happy she was pregnant."

"How would you know that, if she hadn't told anyone she was pregnant?" I was shocked. Though H had spoke of his past very little, sometimes when alcohol was in his system he'd opened up, and he'd always spoken of how in love he and his wife were and how they'd been so excited about the baby they'd been expecting.

"My mom told me that Vee kept a diary. Right from being young, she'd written one. My mom went in her room one day before she passed and saw it poking out from under the bed. She'd continued to write in an old one occasionally."

"I see."

"She'd written that she was confused. That Henry had wanted them to try for a baby, but she'd continued taking contraception until a slip up had led to a pregnancy. That he was overjoyed, but that she didn't want to be home with a baby. She loved to work. She wrote that she hadn't yet told anyone else because she didn't want to hear the congratulations because she didn't feel happy about it yet. That she was waiting for the first kicks and then maybe it would all seem more real and she'd become as excited as Henry."

A tear ran down her face.

"My mom feels tremendous guilt that she didn't ask Vee about how she was feeling, instead deciding it was between Vee and Henry. Now I know this, Aidan. I can't tell Henry, it would destroy him."

I sat back and had a sip of wine. "No, there's nothing to be gained at this point by him learning that. It could break him. Maybe one day he'll deserve to know the truth. But not now. I won't say anything, Amelia. You have my word."

"Thank you." She answered. "God, way to ruin a lovely meal, Amelia."

"You haven't ruined anything, and the night is still young." I reassured her and then I regaled her with another story of how I manipulated my way into taking over a business until she was distracted enough that her emotions lessened.

By the time we caught a cab to the club we were loaded, having drunk copious amounts of wine, far too much for the food to have soaked up.

"I thought I'd be nervous, but actually I'm quite excited." Amelia giggled in the cab. "I can't believe I'm going to see people actually having sex."

"Ssh." I warned her, though I knew the cab driver would be aware of the clubs in the city. "It's a private club; you need to keep your voice down."

"Oops." She giggled again, and I wondered if I'd made a mistake in bringing her here tonight. I prayed it was nerves, rather than alcohol that was causing the laughter.

I showed my key on the way in and booked in Amelia as a guest under a made up name. As the woman on the desk knew me well, she didn't check who I was bringing with me. Usually guests had to go through a series of verifications. I took hold of Amelia's hand and dragged her along with me as she stared at the black decor with the silver stars. We went up in the lift and then out into the reception area and through to the main bar. Amelia walked in and took a seat at an empty table.

"I don't know what I was expecting." She said. "But this is just a normal bar. I thought people would be fucking in the middle of the floor."

The word 'fucking' sounded alien on her tongue and I had to remind myself that she was a grown woman of twenty-three. "It does happen when the show takes place at midnight," I told her. I went on to explain that each night either an auction took place, or the stage was hired out by anyone who wanted to put on a show or live out a fantasy. At that point anything went in the main bar, but until that time the main bar area was kept for drinking only. Anyone wanting to do more went through to the side rooms, where they could choose a colored wristband depending on whether they wanted to observe or were willing to join in with any play.

"Can we go through? Please?" Begged Amelia.

"Sure. As long as you promise not to giggle." I told her.

She mimed her mouth being closed.

"Okay, so make sure you accept a white wristband that shows to the others that you are only there to observe. Otherwise a pretty young blonde like you is going to be mobbed."

She nodded and followed me to the edge of the room where we walked through a door marked by the presence of a security guard. We both placed the observer wristbands on our wrists and began to walk down the corridor. Amelia's eyes widened as she stared through the first window where a woman was deep-throating a man as another man watched.

"Oh my god," she whispered.

Slowly, she walked the full length of the room, taking in the various scenes in front of her. "Have you done this?" She asked me. "Have you ever taken part?"

"Many times." I admitted. I took a deep breath. "And sometimes H and I team up to satisfy a woman."

I witnessed Amelia tremble. "Wh-what did you just say?"

"H didn't want another relationship, but he still needed sex. He found the club. He bought it afterward. We sometimes help a woman live out her fantasies of two men at once. One in her pussy and one in her mouth or her ass."

"I, I-"

"What, Amelia? Did you really think H owned a sex club and never participated?"

"I honestly don't know what I thought."

Amelia didn't run. It surprised me. I thought faced with the reality of the club and discovering H wasn't the idyllic Prince Charming of her childhood imagination, she would bolt. It reassured me. Instead, she carried on watching, fascinated with the scenes being played out in front of her.

"Are you okay?" I asked her.

"I'm fine, Aiden. I'm doing what you recommended. I'm seeing if any of these scenarios speak to me. See if there's anything I'd maybe one day want to try."

Oh fuck. If H found out I brought her here, and it led to a subsequent descent into debauchery, he was going to kick my ass.

Amelia carried on looking around and when the siren went off, we went and watched the stage show. As I drove her home, she seemed subdued and lost in thought, though she had exhausted me with a seemingly never-ending series of questions.

The cab drew up outside H's apartment.

"Thank you, Aidan." She leaned over and kissed me on the cheek. "Thank you for not treating me like a child, and for showing me around the club. I'm so sick of everyone trying to protect me. Acting like I'm some innocent little teenager, and not a grown woman."

"You're welcome." I told her, and I watched as she got out of the cab and went home.

CHAPTER SEVEN

Amelia

What an evening!

My mind whirled with all the experiences of the day and night. Aidan had been fantastic company though I knew I had friend-zoned him. Hey, if you didn't get horny for a guy while standing at the side of him while people had sex in front of you, it wasn't going to happen!

I pushed open the door of the apartment and shook my foot so that one heeled shoe came off and then repeated the movement with my other foot.

A door opened. "What's all the fucking noise? Some of us are trying to sleep here."

"Henry? I thought you were away until tomorrow?" I stood frozen in the doorway while my mind caught up with reality.

"It finished early, and I decided I'd rather be home. Where have you been anyway until this hour? Have you been drinking?"

I began to walk down the corridor toward him, my path a little haphazard as the alcohol messed with my equilibrium.

"I might have had a little drink." I said, holding my finger and thumb about an inch apart.

Henry leaned against the door jamb. He was wearing pajamas, and his pajama shirt wasn't fastened. I could see a little of his chest. I wanted to see more damn it.

"A little drink, right." Henry's mouth curled at the edges.

I stood and placed my hands across my chest. "Are you laughing at me?"

"So, where did you go?" He asked me. "And who with?"

I placed a finger on my nose. "I'm not telling you where I went, Mr. Nosy. It's a secret."

Henry sighed and moved away from the door. "Night, Amelia. I'll talk to you in the morning."

"You have a lovely chest." It was out of my mouth before I could register that I'd said it aloud.

I saw Henry hold himself taut. It just made his ripped chest even more delectable.

I wet my bottom lip with my tongue. I couldn't help myself.

"Sorry about that." I said. "But you just put it in front of me, all bare, and I'm just a woman with eyes. I have really good vision and I saw it. Oops."

My cell phone flashed, and I dug it out of my purse, but then dropped it on the floor.

Henry bent down and picked it up while I was still trying to work out how I could bend over without falling.

"You have a message from Aidan." He bit out. "Letting you know he arrived home safely."

I took my cell off him and put it back in my purse, which I then dropped on the floor. Screw it, I'd pick it up in the morning.

He grabbed hold of my arm. "Are you dating Aidan?"

"No." I shook my arm away from his hold. "But if I was, what has it got to do with you?"

"Fuck this." He said and stepping in front of me and putting a hand behind my waist, he backed me to the wall next to his bedroom door.

His lips crashed onto mine and despite my drunken haze, I felt and experienced every single sensation that the kiss delivered. Goose bumps sprang up on my neck and along my arms. My panties, still damp from the club experience, were in danger of becoming sodden. I placed my arms up around his neck and gave myself up to the kiss. His tongue entered my mouth, dancing with my own. I felt my nipples harden and I let out a moan. Then his lips left mine as I was held at arms-length.

"What the fuck am I doing? My God, Amelia. I am so fucking sorry."

"No." I screamed. "Do not be fucking sorry for kissing me. It was amazing."

"You're drunk. I took advantage. Go to bed, Amelia, please." He begged, his eyes now full of panic, instead of the lust that had burned there just seconds before.

Suddenly feeling very sober, I turned away from him and walked further down the corridor to my own room. I heard his door close as I walked. Remembering the kiss, I raised my fingers and brushed them across my lips. It had been everything I'd ever dreamed about and more. I thought I would have felt guilt about Vee. That I'd kissed my sister's husband. But I didn't. For a moment Henry had come alive again, with his lips fastened on my own. He'd wanted me. He'd been jealous of Aidan and he'd wanted me, and as far as I knew, he wasn't drunk.

Elated, I pushed open the door of my room, and accidentally slamming it shut behind me, I slumped onto my bed still dressed in my short black dress. I hitched it up around my waist exposing my panties and then I dipped my fingers under the edge of them until I could feel my slick warmth. I was so wet! I thought about what I'd seen at the club and then I thought about my kiss with Henry. In my mind Henry was in one of the rooms at the club and I was there too. He kissed me deeply and then his hand went inside my pants and he strummed my clit. My juices poured for him. I wanted him in me so goddamn badly. I quickly pulled off my panties and threw them off the bed and then I widened my legs apart, returning my fingers to my pussy and my brain to my fantasy. Back in my imagination, I lowered Henry's pants and removed his boxers and took in the sight of his impressive cock. Then as I laid back against the bed in one of the rooms at Club S, he had lined his cock up against my entrance and thrust inside me. Back in my room, I thrust two fingers inside myself from one hand while my thumb brushed against my clit and I imagined he was fucking me.

"Oh my God, yes. Yes."

And I came, wave after glorious wave coursing through my body, resulting in me feeling so relaxed I fell asleep with one last thought in my mind.

Could Henry Carter be the one who I actually managed to have sex with?

As the sun streamed through my opened drapes, I woke and almost hissed. Oh my god, my head! I looked down at myself, taking in the dress around my waist and my bare pussy, and I flushed with embarrassment. What on earth was happening to me? Did I have no shame? I looked at my bedside alarm clock, six-fifteen am. My alarm was due to go off in five minutes time. Oh please no. Having decided that a shower, plus coffee, was the answer, I slowly shuffled myself out of bed and padded over to my en-suite where I set the temperature to a pleasant heat and once under the faucet, turned it up even hotter so it soothed my body. I had the jets trained on the back of my neck trying to alleviate the tension that was there every time I thought about the fact that Henry and I had kissed. If I went for my breakfast at this time, there was a large chance I'd see him. Maybe I'd be better staying in my room until the coast was clear? However, once I was out of the shower and dressed, and had towel dried my hair, my need for coffee was huge. I walked down to the kitchen and winced once again as my eyes were assaulted by the sunny day.

Mary turned to me and laughed.

"Looks like someone had a good night?" She poured me a large mug of fresh coffee and handed it to me, first adding a splash of cold water so I could start drinking it immediately. I took a gulp. My mouth wanted to scream hallelujah at the liquid refreshment that was lubricating my throat.

"I went out for dinner with a colleague and we drank rather too much wine. We went on to a club and there he had a membership where drinks were inclusive. Mary, I've never drunk so much in my life."

She chuckled. "And was this *colleague* handsome?"

"Yes, but he's not for me." I scrunched up my nose. I looked around the kitchen. "Henry not up yet?"

"Henry left at six this morning as I was just arriving." Mary answered, and I knew my face was wracked with disappointment and unease. I'd not expected him to do that, and so I didn't have a chance to put my game face on.

"His face looked like thunder and when I asked him if everything was okay, he said he had to be in the office early as he had an appointment with Aidan Hall and needed to prepare for it."

Oh shit.

"But now I've seen your face, I can see there's obviously something that's happened that I'm not privy too. Is Henry in any trouble?"

I noted how she had started calling him Henry of late and how Henry hadn't corrected her. Then I saw she was staring at me and waiting for an answer to her question.

I sighed. A girl needed someone to talk to and Mary was turning out to be a good listener and adviser.

"You aren't allowed to say anything."

"My lips are sealed." Mary mimed the motion of pulling a zip across her mouth, and then her face launched into a look like she had all the inside gossip on the Kardashian/Jenner family.

"So the man I went to dinner with last night..."

"Was Aidan Hall?" She interrupted.

"Yes."

She squealed. "Now it all makes sense. That's why Henry is so pissed. He's jealous."

"I don't know." I replied. "But last night when I arrived home, he kissed me."

Mary's mouth fell open, "He did?"

I nodded. "Yes, but then he said it was a huge mistake and basically closed his door in my face."

Mary looked thoughtful. "I should imagine he's feeling all kinds of guilt, especially as he was married to your sister. He'll also be wondering what your family would think if they found out."

I shrugged. "They loved Henry. I'd like to think that after the shock had settled, they'd accept it."

"So you've thought about a future with him?"

"Not with any seriousness. I never actually thought something would happen between us. I just thought I'd meet someone else and live happily ever after with them one day. That I'd get my own Prince Henry but it wouldn't be Henry, if you get what I'm saying." I sighed.

"But you came here to see if there was a possibility?"

"I guess so," I confessed. "Deep down inside I can't deny it was an idea."

"Well, I guess my advice is that you're going to have to be patient." She offered. "The fact he left early to go charging to deal with your dinner date is encouraging."

"Shit, Aidan! I'd better send him a warning text," I said.

"You'll need this, then?" Mary met my look of confusion with her hand, waving my purse in my face.

"Where did I leave that?"

"Middle of the hallway, along with your shoes."

"Jesus, I really did have a good night."

I took out my cell and fired a quick message to Aidan.

Amelia: Henry knows we went for dinner, but that's all. He left in a temper, apparently.

A text came back within a minute.

Aidan: I can handle Henry Carter. Been doing it for years. I think I should call at your office for coffee afterward and we should record his reaction on our cell phones.

Amelia: You are so evil. Be careful!

I put my cell back in my purse and drank down the rest of my coffee.

"God, that feels so much better. I don't know what I would do without you, Mary."

"Bacon sandwich to go?"

"Actually I think it's you I love," I told her and then we both gasped.

What the hell had I just said?

"And on that rather embarrassing note, I'll go fix my hair and makeup." I jumped down off my stool and practically ran to my room.

Love?

I loved him?

Impossible. I hardly knew him. It was infatuation, pure and simple.

But maybe it could lead to love.

I decided that I'd had enough of acting like a lovesick teenager and I had a job to get to. It was time to kick some ass in the world of property.

Having eaten a bacon sandwich in the car before I drove to work, by the time I got to the office and passed Jessica, the salt had made my mouth like the Sahara desert.

"I need coffee, stat!" I begged her.

"Coming right up." She grabbed her purse.

When she returned, she brought in two cups and I looked at her strangely. "Do I have an appointment this morning?"

"No, just a hangover, and so I thought one cup might not be enough."

"You are the best assistant I ever had." I told her.

"I am indeed an amazing assistant." She agreed. "Are you ready for your messages?"

"Fire away."

"So, the property you are going to visit at one pm is now with Green's realtors."

"Ooh, gossip there?"

"Well it was with Simpson's until this morning, and then all of a sudden there was a change, so someone wasn't happy."

"So, who am I meeting now?" I asked.

"A realtor called Tiffany Bailey. She's lovely. I've spoken to her many a time on the phone. You'll have to tell me what she's like in real life."

"I will do." I smiled.

Jessica ran through the rest of my messages.

"Thanks so much, Jessica. Anything else?" I asked before she left the room.

"I don't know what happened with Mr. Carter and Mr. Hall first thing, but Mr. Hall left saying that

Mr. Carter needed to get his head out of his ass so he could stop talking shit and see what was in front of him." She bit her lip, obviously unsure if she should have shared.

"Oooh, I like it. Boy fight. Maybe next time they could mud wrestle?" I winked.

CHAPTER EIGHT

Henry

Lust.

Guilt.

Frustration.

Temptation.

Confusion.

I didn't get even five minutes of sleep. Exhaustion wanted to take hold of my body, but my whirling brain wouldn't allow it. Eventually I gave up and worked from my laptop. Figured I might as well achieve something and attempt to distract myself at the same time.

I fucking kissed her.

Totally crossed a line.

And what the hell was Aidan playing at? I told him to leave her alone. So, he takes her out to dinner?

When five am hit, I slipped out of the house and hit the gym, stretching and pushing my body and finishing with a cold shower. Adrenaline now pumped through my veins and I hoped it would see me through the day. I went back to the apartment and fixed myself a large coffee, then grabbed everything I needed for work.

I was just headed on my way out of the door when I heard a key and Mary pushed the door open. She startled.

"Oh, my, Henry. You made me jump."

Henry? She'd started calling me Henry a few days ago. Things were changing way too fast for me right now. I needed to escape.

"Sorry, Mary. I gotta run. Busy day ahead."

"It must be if you're setting off this early. Do you not have time for a quick breakfast, or have you already eaten?" Her brows knitted together with a look of concern.

"Grabbed a coffee, but I have an early meeting with Aidan Hall, so I need to move my ass. I'll get

THE BILLIONAIRE AND THE VIRGIN

Ashley to get us some breakfast, as I doubt he'll have eaten either."

"You men need to look after yourselves better. You'll be sending yourselves into an early grave." She said. Then she looked at me, guiltily. Christ, everything came down to me being a widower. The tragic man who lost his wife young.

And who's to blame for that? My inner voice chastised me.

"I'll be back before you leave," I promised Mary, for reasons I didn't know.

She nodded, wished me a good day and then I was out the door.

A iden walked into the office cool as fuck.
"Morning, bro. How's the corporate world?"

"Yeah, fuck that. What are you playing at with Amelia?"

Aidan had the audacity to smirk. "Why, H, you're very overprotective about your *employee*. Sure there's not another reason why you're banning me from pursuing her?"

"She's like family."

"Stop bullshitting us both, H. You like her. It's

written all over your face. You look like you want to tear me limb from limb and I only took her out on a business dinner. This has nothing to do with her working for you, or her being any kind of family. The way I see it, you want her, and she wants you. So what's the fucking problem? Live your life, H. Date the girl, fuck the girl. Go and do it before someone beats you to it."

I thumped the desk. "You're way out of fucking line."

"Someone's got to be. I spoke to her. She might be twenty-three but she's naive, innocent. She's working in the world of billionaires; you think one of them isn't going to take a shine, an interest, in the hot young blonde? Get over yourself. You've played the suffering widower card long enough. We've all had shit in our life, H. All of us. My brother died when I was fourteen."

My mouth dropped open.

"Yeah, you didn't know that. Motorcycle acci-dent. First thing I did, learned to ride a fucking bike when I was old enough to say 'fuck you' to the universe. Can't say my mom was thrilled but she said, and I quote, 'Honey, when the Lord decides it's your time, he's going to take you if you're on a bike or a fluffy cloud of cotton wool." I see his taut jaw. I don't think I've ever seen Aidan this pissed.

"If there is a God up there, he must be pissed with you right now, wasting your precious life. Now I'm telling you, man. Make a move on that woman if you want to, and if not, back off, because she can date who she chooses to date. It has nothing to do with you. You aren't family. You were married to her sister and barely knew the girl herself. Now are you getting us some coffee and breakfast, so we can talk business, or do I need to come over there and beat the shit out of you first?"

I sat back in my chair and buzzed through to reception.

"Coffees and a breakfast selection please."

"Coming right up, Mr. Carter."

I leaned back in my chair.

"I kissed Amelia last night." I confessed.

"You did what? Why didn't you say so in the first place? I wouldn't have made my speech if I'd known you'd already made a move."

"I told her it was a mistake, and I went back to my room."

Aidan places his head in his hands. "You fucked up."

"I was confused. This is all so new to me. I've

had no proper relationships since Veronica. Just the acquaintances at the club and whatever the hell you'd class the three-way with Tiffany and Brandon as."

"Well, I personally would class it as you were almost ready to date again but then you wimped out and added Brandon to the mix. Of course, she then went on to fall madly in love with Brandon and you got kicked to the curb."

"Maybe."

"What if she hadn't been interested in Brandon? What if she'd only wanted to see you?"

"I'd have ended it. I was fond of her, but it wasn't love."

"And are you fond of Amelia?"

"I'm confused as fuck about Amelia. I feel like I've known her forever, and she's changing things. Everywhere she goes, something about my life changes. People are calling me fucking Henry. I'm starting to become approachable and I've even smiled at people. I'm becoming a pussy."

"Or you're finally starting to live life again? Look no one is putting a time pressure on you. See where things go with Amelia. Start out as friends if you need to. Just don't hurt her. Like I say, she's innocent, very innocent."

There's something about the way he says that word that sets alarm bells ringing in my head.

"What are you getting at?"

He sighed. "She asked me not to say anything so don't you dare fucking say this came from me."

"Spill."

"She's a virgin."

A knock sounded on the door and the receptionist entered with our drinks and breakfast before leaving us in peace. It gave me the few minutes I needed to be able to breathe again.

"She's twenty-three."

"She says she's never been relaxed enough to go the whole way."

"And how the ever loving fuck did this come up in conversation? Were you trying to make a move on her?"

"How many more times? I'm not trying to make a move on Amelia. We were chatting. We get on well. As friends." He said those last two words to me slowly. "And I intend to stay her friend, so you can quit with your macho posturing. Anyway, you need to apologize to the woman for last night. God only knows what a state she's in this morning. Where is she anyway?"

I type into my electronic diary and tap over onto

Amelia's calendar.

"She's checking out a new condo development. Oh, fuck."

"What?"

"The realtor changed. She's meeting Tiffany."

CHAPTER NINE

Amelia

I was out at a new development in Manhattan that Henry wanted to purchase and turn around for a huge profit. The place was still being built, so I had arranged to meet the realtor, Tiffany, at a nearby coffee shop.

I arrived and looked around, spotting a small, pretty blonde-haired woman near the counter. She turned to me and smiled, and I realized she was expecting a baby. "Amelia?" She asked.

"Yes." I replied, and we shook hands.

"What would you like? My treat. Just please don't tell my gym instructor husband that I ate both a cookie and a donut."

I laughed. I liked her already.

"I promise. Two goodies sounds great. I'll copy you, if that's okay? I had a late night. I need plenty of coffee this morning."

She placed our orders, and we went and took a seat each at a table by the window.

"Are you in a rush or shall we enjoy our coffees first, and then I'll go through the particulars with you and then show you around?"

"That sounds great. I'm in no rush to get back to the office." This was true. I was in no rush to bump into Henry any time soon. I had to face up to the fact that he may want me to move out of the apartment now, even quit my job. Goddamn it. What the fuck was I going to do if we'd messed everything up?

"You look like you've a lot on your mind there, girl. You okay?"

"Yeah," I sigh, "It's nothing important."

"Man trouble. I can smell it a mile off." She smiled. "I used to share an apartment with two other women. I've seen that face so many times, on my own reflection and on my roommates'."

"Mine is a lack of man trouble." I giggled.

"Oh, I suffered from that in the past too. Or they were complete dicks."

"But I guess now you're happy?" I pointed to her stomach.

"Yes, married, madly in love with my gorgeous husband, and five months pregnant. I'm due in May."

"Aww, congratulations, Tiffany."

"Thank you. Oh and please call me Tiff, that's what my friends call me." She beamed. "So, how's the new job going?"

"It's early days, but I'm enjoying it so far."

"And I hear you were H's wife's younger sister?"

"News certainly travels fast around here." I smiled before explaining. "Yeah, I'm Vee's younger sister. A lot younger. I didn't know Henry that well."

"I'm not sure anyone knows him that well," she said.

"Have you worked in the same circles as Henry for long?" I asked her.

"I met him back in 2016," She said, "When I showed him a condo."

"Once seen, never forgotten, hey?" I joked.

"Something like that." She smiled. She looked uncomfortable, so I changed the subject back to her husband.

"Did you know with Brandon that he was the

one?" I asked. "Is that a real thing, or is it made up fairy tale shit?"

"Okay, I'm gonna be dead honest here and it might shock you a little, but I'm not ashamed of my past."

I looked warily at her, "Please don't feel you have to answer me. I'm sorry. We only just met."

"Yeah, but I've a feeling we're gonna be friends." She smiled. "I was seeing H when I met Brandon."

I took a sharp intake of breath. "I thought he didn't date?"

"Oh, I wouldn't call it dating. We hooked up. Then I met Brandon and well, I fell in love with him."

"So what did Henry say to that?" My heart was thudding in my chest.

"It turned out that H had arranged for Brandon to move in across from me, with a plan for him to take me on a date and stop me developing any feelings for H himself." She scoffed. "If I hadn't fallen in love with Brandon, I'd have killed them both."

"Well, I guess I'm not shocked that Henry would do that. He seems to avoid anything that could resemble a relationship."

"Oh, that's not the shocking part." She replied.

"The shocking part is we went on to have a ménage relationship for a year."

The rest of the meeting with Tiff passed in a blur. Although I'd said all the right things to her, and even managed to make out I was completely intrigued by the whole ménage thing, I couldn't get away from the fact that she'd enjoyed a sexual relationship with Henry. He'd been inside her. He'd made her come. She'd had his naked body against hers. We'd talked about Club S, and I told her I'd visited there to observe.

By the time I got back to the office, I was in a fiery mood. Henry had left early, no doubt to avoid me further because when the hell had he ever left early before? From what Mary had told me he was a workaholic. I made some notes on the computer about my meeting today and made some phone calls in connection with the business.

The more I thought about last night and then meeting Tiffany, the more incensed I became. Maybe I should just pack up and give up. He'd told me nothing about his life with my sister and the kiss had complicated everything. I thought about the life he led at the club, the ménages. My God, if he slept with me and found out I was a virgin, he would want to laugh anyway. My inexperience would be a complete embarrassment alongside his vast sexual knowledge. Having my v-card now really sucked. There was only one thing for it. I needed to lose it. I would go to Club S and I would take part until the stupid thing had gone. Maybe I wouldn't lose it there, perhaps I'd just meet someone and go back to a hotel room, but I needed it gone. I called Aidan.

"I want to go back to Club S tonight. Can you get me in again?"

"What's the rush to go back there?"

Shit. I needed something that would sound plausible.

"I think it helped me relax around sex being there, just watching. Broke down some barriers, I guess."

"But you're not considering taking part?"

"No," I lied, "Of course not."

"I'll pick you up at nine."

"No, I'll make my own way there. I don't want Henry to see you and start trouble again."

"I've spoken to Henry, he's fine."

"Oh?"

"Yeah, I think he wants to speak to you. Hopefully, he'll apologize for being an alpha male."

I had no intention of going to Henry's tonight. I planned to go shopping for an outfit, and I'd grab something to eat while I was out. Then I'd come back to the office and get changed there.

"I'll meet you out front at nine thirty." I told him. It was a shame there wasn't some way of sneaking up there from this floor. Instead I had to go all the way to the lobby for the magic key that would bring me back up to the twenty-fourth floor.

A idan met me as planned. He looked uneasy.

"I'm not sure about this, Amelia. You're up to something."

"I'm twenty-three years old. So what if I was? I didn't have time to get a membership arranged today. Either you can get me in, or I'll go to a club somewhere else and pick someone up. It doesn't have to happen at Club S."

"I knew it. This is about your virginity, isn't it?"

"Keep your voice down, for God's sake," I hissed.

"I'll get you in because like you said you're a grown woman, but I'm asking you, Amelia, to not do anything stupid tonight. Please go talk to Henry. You both need to sit and discuss what happened last night."

"There's nothing to discuss. He rejected me. He's obviously not interested in me."

"He's scared of being hurt."

"He wasn't scared of screwing Tiffany." I spat out.

Aidan went quiet. "You found that out, huh?"

"He couldn't deal with the potential relationship, so he set her up with someone else. I realize now that he's beyond help. Now, please will you get me in?"

Aidan sighed, but walked up to the reception and booked us both in.

"I'll escort you to the bar, stay for a drink and then I'm out of there."

"Thank you."

"I hope you know what you're doing." He said, and he looked at me with disappointment. Tonight was the first time Aidan had not met me with his usual endearing smile, and I shook off the feelings of uncertainty that were starting to flood through me.

After drinking a scotch, Aidan kissed me on the cheek and left. I remained sitting at the bar in my tight silver dress that fitted to my skin like a glove. Sheer black stockings and a high pair of black heeled shoes completed my look.

Grabbing my bottle of wine and a glass, I hopped

down off my stool and went through to the rooms, once again placing an observer band on my wrist. The next thirty minutes were spent watching people losing themselves to lust. I tried to focus on the women, how they were able to let themselves go, to relax in the moment. They were lost to the pleasure. It was easy to see that my problem had stemmed from the fact that my previous lovers hadn't taken me to that level. I'd been focused on it hurting, the potential pain, instead of being delirious about chasing an orgasm and the feeling of utmost pleasure. I wanted in. I wanted to feel what they felt. Emboldened by a few glasses of wine, I went back up to the doorman, removed my white wristband and picked up a black one with the silver stars. It was time to play.

I walked back over to the windows, moving down them one at a time, trying to decide which room, which scene I was willing to try to join.

"Good evening." A man you'd describe as a silver fox had walked over to me. He took my hand in his. "I'm Anthony, and what do I call this delightful creature in front of me?"

"Off fucking limits," A gruff voice barked out from behind me. Then my arm was held in a stiff grip, and I was pulled away from Mr. Fox.

Henry's steely eyes burned through me. "What the fuck are you doing, Amelia?"

"How did you know I was here?" I asked, then I shook my head. "Aidan. Aidan fucking called you, didn't he?"

"Yes. He was terrified you were making the biggest mistake of your life."

"I wish everyone would mind their own business about how I conduct my love life."

"Why are you here, Amelia? Answer my question truthfully and I will go home and leave you here to do whatever you want." He took a deep breath. "Are you here because of me? Because you think I don't want you?"

My shoulders stiffened. "I'm not experienced enough for you, Henry. I'm moving on."

"Like fuck you are." He said. "You want to lose that innocence? Then you'll fucking do it with me. You hear me? No one else. Just me." He held up my arm, pulled off the band and threw it across the room.

"We're going home. Do you have a problem with that? I'm taking you to my bedroom and we're going to fuck. I don't care if it takes all night or the next three days. We're not leaving that room until you're no longer a virgin. If you're not interested, now is the time to walk away. I'll take you home to get your belongings and I'll pay for you to stay in a hotel. Which is it to be, Amelia?"

I bit my lip. Was this really happening right now?

"I want you to fuck me, Henry."

Then I was whisked from that room so fast my head span.

The car ride home was steeped with tension and silence. Henry was completely focused on getting us home safely. I sat beside him wondering if he would have calmed down and changed his mind by the time we were through the doorway.

"No, I've not changed my mind. I'm rock hard for you, Amelia." He'd read my expression.

"Okay." I replied. My heart felt like it was going to beat right out of my chest.

We pulled up outside the apartment and Henry opened the door. Once through he picked me up and kicking the door behind him, marched us off to his bedroom.

CHAPTER TEN

Henry

I was so fucking tired that I did something I didn't remember doing for a long, long time. I took the afternoon off to go home and sleep. Tonight I needed to talk to Amelia, and I couldn't do that on no sleep. I sent Mary home when I got back so that the apartment would be quiet and then I hit the sack and slept for hours, overcome by everything that had been happening.

Later the sound of my cell phone woke me. I was going to ignore it at first, but then I remembered I'd abandoned the office and there was a chance someone needed me. It was Aidan. "Carter." I answered.

"Henry, Amelia is at Club S."

"She's what?" I was wide awake in seconds. "How the fuck did she find out about the club?"

"She already knew about it. Anyway, there's no time for me to explain. She's in there and the way she was talking makes me think she's considering losing her innocence there. It's really not the place for that to happen. What do you want me to do? She told me to mind my own business."

"I'm on my way. I'll sort it. Speak later." I told him. I ended the call and thanked God I'd fallen asleep with my clothes on. I grabbed my keys and set off for the club.

Once inside, I scanned the bar, but there was no sign of her. My heart beat hard in my chest as I made my way to the side rooms and prayed that I wasn't going to find her in there with another man. Oh I knew my own past, I didn't need reminding I'd fucked my way around this club. But this was a place to play. It was no place for an innocent girl to come to lose her virginity.

The minute I went through to the rooms, I saw her. I watched as she stared through the windows watching the scenes. She was wearing a tight silver dress that showed off her amazing tits and ass, and high black heels that emphasized the curve of her calves. I wanted to run my lips up those curves, all the way up those thighs and past those tits until I was back kissing that mouth. Then a man appeared in front of her. He held out his hand for her to shake. As she placed her hand in his I saw she was wearing a black and silver band on her wrist. The one that said she was available to play.

Like hell she was.

I made my way over to her, determined to bring her home.

And that's where we were now. I dropped her down onto my bed and I stripped myself out of all my clothes. Her blue eyes followed me every step of the way, but there was no fear in her gaze, no apprehension, only hunger. I pulled down my boxers revealing my massive cock, and she gasped. I was huge, and she was going to enjoy every bit of it.

"We're in no rush, Amelia. By the time my cock is seeking entrance you're going to be begging me for it." I told her.

I pulled off each stiletto and threw them to the floor. Then I lifted her right foot and ran my tongue along the sole. She whimpered as it tickled slightly and she tried to pull her foot away. Her skin tasted salty on my tongue. I repeated the same to her left foot and then placing her feet back on the bed, I lifted the bottom of her dress, revealing those black hold up stockings that were encasing creamy thighs. I rolled down each stocking in turn, discarded them and then I returned to my ministrations, running my tongue from her ankle, all the way up her leg and right to the crux of her thigh at the side of her panties. I could see that the white panties she was wearing were damp, and I broke off from what I was doing.

"That wetness better be for me, Amelia, and not for the people at the club." She squirmed. "Did watching people at the club make you wet? Tell me the truth." I commanded.

"A little, but mainly I looked at them and thought of it being you."

"You looked at sexual acts and pretended it was me doing them to you?"

"Yes," she groaned, her thighs rubbing together.

"And what did you see? What did you imagine I was doing to you?"

"That you had your fingers inside me, your tongue, your-" She broke off.

"Say it, Amelia."

"Your cock. That you had your cock in me and made me come."

I returned to her other ankle, and I tongued from her ankle right up to the juncture of her thighs again.

"God, Henry, please touch me." She begged.

"All in good time, Amelia." I told her.

I sat astride her and pulled up her dress, taking it over her head and dropping it at my side. Then Amelia was laid under me in just her bra and panties. Her creamy breasts spilled out over the top of her bra and I began my teasing again, trailing my tongue up the side of her waist, over the curve of her breasts, making her push out her chest, and then back down the other side.

I trailed my mouth up the curve of her neck causing goosebumps to break out over her skin, and then I devoured her mouth with my own. The kiss went on and on. I had no rush to leave her mouth. All I knew was that something was happening tonight, something different. I had slept with many women but there was something about Amelia, it was like she messed with my internal systems, set forth some kind of electrical charge. My whole body was on fire for her. Finally, I broke the kiss and unhooked her bra revealing those amazing breasts. I dipped my head to lave one nipple and then the other while soft moans emitted from Amelia's mouth.

I trailed my fingers down her body until I reached those soaked panties and then I dipped my hand under the edge of them and took in her warm heat.

"Fuck." I wanted nothing more than to ram my rock hard cock inside her but I needed patience. Instead I rubbed her wetness around her clit and dipped my finger in and out of her. I'd expected her to tense up, but she hadn't. She was rolling her hips up in rhythm with my finger fucking. I added a further finger. She was tight, I wouldn't add another at the moment, but I continued to rock against her as she continued to rock back.

"Oh my god, Henry, oh my god."

I felt her quicken around my fingers and then moisture seeped from her sweet cunt as she spasmed around my digits. Her whole body trembled, her breathing making her body shake as she came down from her orgasm.

"Did you enjoy that?" I asked her.

She nodded eagerly. My sweet, beautiful, willing, Amelia.

I kissed her again until she'd had time to recover and then I lowered myself between her thighs. She screamed my name as I licked up her seam, then teased her bud. I tongue-fucked her slowly until she was begging me. "Please, Henry, please."

I moved up the bed and raised myself above her. "I'm going to fuck you now, Amelia. Try to relax. If it doesn't happen, we try again in a while, okay? It's not a race."

I lined my cock against her entrance and I started to push myself against her. Immediately she tightened up like a vice.

I dropped back down between her legs and licked and teased her pussy until she was once again relaxed and on the edge of orgasm.

I returned above her. "I'm just going to rub myself against you, so you get used to me being there. I'm not going to do anything, okay?"

"Yes," she replied. "Okay."

I rubbed my cock between her sweet wet folds over and over until eventually she started rubbing herself back against me, trying to seek an orgasm. I pushed slightly at her center and she accepted the first part of me.

"I'm in you." I told her.

Her closed eyes fluttered open. "You are?"

"Yes, only a little, but I'm there. Can you feel me?"

ANGEL DEVLIN

It was as if telling her she'd already done it helped, as she continued to relax as I rocked my hips a little further giving her an inch of myself at a time. Then I came up against her barrier of resistance, her virginity. I paused, kissed her mouth and then looked into her eyes. "It's going to hurt a little." I told her. "At least, that's what I hear."

"You never slept with a virgin before?" She asked me.

I shook my head, "No, so you see, it's my first time too."

She laughed heartily at this. "Henry is a virgin with virgins. I feel special."

"You are special." I said and those blue eyes met mine once again. She was so innocent.

I pushed past her barrier and she winced slightly. "Is it too painful?" I asked.

"Carry on, please." She said.

I did. I carried on inch by inch until she had the majority of my cock in her pussy and then I began to move. I knew she'd get little from this fuck, so I rocked inside her gently until I felt my balls tighten and I spilled my seed inside her.

I withdrew and pulled her into my arms on the bed.

"You're no longer a virgin," I told her, as I

122

grabbed a tissue from the side of the bed and wiped between her thighs, showing her the small bloody evidence of the loss of her innocence.

"Thank fuck for that." She said. "I know it'll get better with practice." She said.

"Oh you can bet your sweet ass it will," I told her.

I woke her up again at three am and five am to 'practice' and this time, although sore, she came around my cock both times. At six thirty am I woke up to find her warm mouth wrapped around my dick. She knew exactly what she was doing with oral sex. She may have been a virgin, but she wasn't inexperienced in using her mouth to pleasure a man. By the time the alarm sounded for us to get ready for work, I wondered if I was going to have to pull another afternoon sickie to come home for a sleep.

I stared at her as she tried to pull herself awake. Her eyes looked at mine and there was a clear fear in them. I knew what she was thinking. That I'd reject her again, tell her I'd made a mistake.

"Amelia." I said to her.

"It's okay." She said.

"No," I stated firmly. "That's not what I'm going to say. I'll start again. Amelia, it has taken me a long, long time to believe I could ever have a relationship with someone else. I'll be honest, I thought it would never happen again. But I feel something for you. It's too early for me to think about what this means, but I'm not going anywhere. I want to explore it with you. I know we need to address the elephant in the room at some point because there's a ghost to lay to rest. But, I'm ready and willing to try, if you are."

Amelia beamed at me. A big beautiful smile swept across her face.

"Oh, I'm ready and willing all right." She winked.

Goddamn it, I had to have her again.

We showered in our separate rooms and then headed down for breakfast from there. When I arrived, Amelia was already sitting at the table nursing a coffee with a fully cooked breakfast in front of her. I watched as Mary loaded up a plate with bacon, eggs and toast and passed it to me.

"You'll need that to help keep your strength up," she said, and winked.

I could have felt embarrassed. Mary had never witnessed any hint of a love affair or even the results of a one-night-stand in the apartment, but instead I decided to go with the flow and with the feeling of happiness-God, yes, happiness-that was coursing through my veins right at that moment.

"Better add another egg and another couple of slices of bacon, Mary." I said to her, and then I winked back.

CHAPTER ELEVEN

Amelia

The next few weeks were heady. It was as if I was living in a dream. We spent every waking moment together, lost in a lust-fueled haze. I craved him inside me, he'd become my drug. I enjoyed work, but I enjoyed it more when Henry came into the office, locked the door and fucked me over the desk.

Today I'd prepared a picnic for us to take over to Central Park. It seemed desperately romantic, and I hoped we would talk about what Henry had described as the 'elephant in the room', my sister. It was time. I was ready to learn about her, other than fleeting bits of information.

After we'd eaten, we sat with our backs against a

tree and Henry started talking. He was no fool, and he'd realized it was time to take things to the next level.

"What do you want to know about Veronica?" He asked.

"Just about you and her. I was too young to take in what she said. I want to know what she was like and what you were like together. You know, where did you meet, etc?"

"We met in a bar. One of my friends was trying to pick her up, and she was having none of it. She said to him that he was wasting his time but that his blond-haired friend would have more of a chance." Henry chuckled. "Luckily, my friend was gracious and introduced us. That was it then, we started dating, then after a year we moved in together. I proposed to her on our two-year anniversary and we married on our third."

"You proposed in a restaurant, right, with musicians playing her favorite song?"

"That's right. It couldn't have gone any better though I was stuttering trying to say the words. Thankfully she accepted."

"Why didn't you have a large wedding? How come you just eloped?"

"She didn't want the fuss. She just wanted to be

Mrs. Carter. She didn't want a honeymoon either. Your sister was a workaholic. We married in the afternoon and if I hadn't booked a hotel room, she'd have gone straight back to the office, I have no doubt in my mind."

I smiled.

He told me many more things about her: her likes and dislikes, and how she said she wished she could spend more time with me. That she looked forward to me being older, so she could show me the business and hopefully see a lot more of me. That she wished Henry had a younger brother.

"She loved you, Amelia. She might not have seen a lot of you, but she loved you. But, in some ways she was as much married to work as she was to me."

"Did that not bother you?"

He shook his head. "No. I knew that from the beginning. It was who she was. Then we discovered she was pregnant. Things were about to change. We talked about her taking some time off from the business. I'd bought us a house back at The Hamptons so she could be near family and your mom could help her with the baby. Don't get me wrong, I wasn't leaving her side, but I figured your mom would show us the ropes. We were clueless, none of our friends had children."

"And then she died."

"Yes. I was showing her the house. She'd had headaches and went into the bathroom. She didn't come back out. I found her slumped on the floor."

His face showed the expression once again of a broken man, and I wrapped my arms around him. I'd been told how my sister had died, but to hear it from the person who found her was so raw and emotional. I couldn't imagine being present in those circumstances.

"After that, everything was gone. My whole future. Gone in the blink of an eye. After the funeral I threw myself into work, into Vee's plans for world domination of the property kingdom. I didn't want another relationship, so one night I ended up at the club. Then I bought it. It became my playground. A place I could get my needs met with no emotional involvement."

"Until Tiffany."

He moved from my arms and sat back against the tree.

"Yes. Until Tiffany." He sighed. "She gave me a hint that maybe it was time to move on. But, I don't know, I couldn't commit. I sent Brandon to her, and they lived happily ever after."

"Did that hurt?"

"No. I was fond of Tiffany. She's a lovely woman and Brandon is a great guy, but I didn't love her. My feelings were confused at first; she was the first woman I had a prolonged relationship with in a long time, but it wasn't a healthy relationship. Ultimately it was still about sex."

He turned to me. "Do you think that's what I'm doing with you? Just fucking?"

I looked across at him. "No, it doesn't feel like that to me. Or am I wrong, and you don't feel the same?"

I do feel the same. He said. "Amelia, I love you."

His words were so unexpected that I burst into tears. This time it was his turn to wrap his arms around me. "Amelia, my Amelia. I didn't mean to make you cry." He told me.

"I-I just never expected to hear those words from you." I confessed. "Henry, I love you too. I think I have from the moment I saw you."

He kissed the tears away from under my eyes and across my cheeks and then his mouth landed on mine.

"Let's go home." He told me.

Home.

That was exactly how it felt, like I'd come home.

· · ·

We went back to the room that was no longer only his, but ours, and stripped out of our clothes. Henry kissed every part of my body, and he took it slow, almost worshiping my skin. He was showing me his love. Showing me that we weren't just fucking. When he finally pushed into me, I wrapped my legs around him and we stared into each other's eyes as we consumed each other with every thrust.

We'd been together for three months when I woke up one morning and the room tilted when I tried to get out of bed. An overwhelming feeling of nausea came over me and I dashed to the bathroom where I emptied the meager contents of my stomach.

"Amelia. Are you okay?" Henry followed me into the bathroom, concern etched across his features.

"Yeah. Just not feeling so good." I said and then I wretched again.

I watched as Henry's face paled. "Amelia, when was your last period?"

Dread filled my stomach. I'd been waiting to come on. My cycle wasn't regular and anywhere between twenty-seven and thirty-one days and I was on day thirty. I was waiting for it.

"I'm due on any day, Henry. I'll just have a virus or something."

"Wipe your mouth and then get back into bed and don't move." He emphasized the words 'don't move' heavily. He quickly dressed. "I'm going to get a test."

Nodding, I crawled back into bed. I felt drained, and no sooner had he left the apartment I fell back to sleep.

When I woke, Henry was at the side of me on the bed.

"Are you feeling better?" He asked.

"A little." I shifted myself slightly, so I was sitting up. "Just feel so nauseous."

"You don't have a headache or anything?"

I turned to Henry, and he was trembling. "No, Henry, I don't." I placed a reassuring hand over his. "Let me go do the test and if it's negative, you can call a doctor for me if it reassures you."

He nodded. "The test is in the bathroom. I bought three different ones, to be certain."

I sat in the bathroom, read the instructions on one of the tests and peed on the stick. Three minutes later the two windows showed me that the test was complete and that I was pregnant. The bathroom door opened, and Henry walked in. "Well?"

"I'm pregnant." I told him, holding up the stick.

"Oh fuck." He said, and he walked back out.

It wasn't the scenario I'd dreamed about as a child, that was for sure.

Henry rang an OB/GYN, pulled strings, and got me an appointment later that day. I was found to be in excellent health with normal symptoms of early pregnancy. It wasn't enough for Henry. He wanted to know if Vee's brain tumor could be genetic, and if I, as her half-sister, could be susceptible. I totally understood his fears, but we already knew the answers. Vee had just been unlucky. There was nothing hereditary about it.

The next few days were a nightmare.

Henry tried to ban me from going to work. It was hard enough when struggling with morning sickness, without Henry constantly following me around. Despite my repeated reassurances that I was all right, he'd snap at me, that I should be resting. The apartment was becoming a prison.

It was ultimately frustration and hormones that called time on things as they stood.

It was a Saturday morning, a week after we'd discovered I was expecting our baby. Pulling on my robe as I sat on the edge of the bed, for once I didn't feel as sick as usual and I decided to get in the shower and then have breakfast on the bedroom balcony facing the park. It felt like a better day.

Stretching, I had risen from the bed and padded into the bathroom. As I walked over to the basin to splash my face, I accidentally kicked the trash can and it fell onto its side with a thud.

The door burst open with such a blast that I screamed.

"Fuck, Amelia, fuck. What was that bang?" Henry looked and saw the trash can on its side.

"Sorry, if I woke you. I kicked it over, being half asleep."

"I thought you'd collapsed." He spat out. "I don't know why you're smiling. There's nothing amusing about any of this."

My temper erupted.

"You're dead right there isn't, Henry. I totally understand your fears but you're out of control. I'm not going to drop dead like Vee. I have a clean bill of health, you had me thoroughly checked out a week ago. Please stop fussing, you are driving me insane."

"Well, sorry I care."

"You're suffocating me, Henry. I feel like utter crap most days and today I've woken feeling okay. I wanted to go enjoy some fresh air and breakfast, and instead I'm dealing with an angry, paranoid man. Has it crossed your mind that this overprotective macho alpha shit isn't good for me, or the baby? Back the hell off, Henry. I'm not Vee."

"Do you get what this is like for me?" Henry shouted, his own temper having combusted. "We were happy. Everything was perfect. I was going to become a dad and then I had nothing."

"Oh my God, Henry. Everything was not perfect. You and Vee weren't some kind of fucking angelic pairing. You were two people in a normal marriage. You've made her a saint since she died. It's a lot to try to live up to. She was just a regular woman."

"We were happy that we were having our baby. We'd got our dream house. Life was so fucking cruel."

"Are you sure about that Henry? Or had you got your dream house? Because the Vee I've learned about wanted to work and wasn't all that enamored about having children."

"Take that back."

"No. The truth hurts, doesn't it, Henry? You wanted her home didn't you, and she didn't want that. She wanted to work. So you bought her a house in The Hamptons near family to try to make sure she was far enough away that she couldn't work. Not until you felt she should go back."

"Where's this coming from, Amelia? Did she tell you this?"

"No. My mom told me about her fucking diary." I told him. "She wrote that she didn't want the baby. That it wasn't the right time. She'd not told any of us she was pregnant. Did you know that?"

Tears fell down Henry's cheeks. "You're a liar. And so unbelievably cruel, and now you're carrying my child. What a goddamn fucked up mess."

He turned and walked out of the bathroom. I heard him get dressed and then he left the apartment and I sat on the bathroom floor and wept.

He was right, what a goddamn fucked up mess.

CHAPTER TWELVE

Henry

I got in my car and drove. My mind knew where I was going. I had Ralph's address in The Hamptons and I knew where it was. I immersed myself in driving. I blocked out everything that had happened, something I had had far too much practice in, and I didn't stop until I pulled up into his driveway, hoping to God he was home.

Ralph answered the door and stood there for a moment staring as if he couldn't believe who was on his doorstep.

He walked out of the doorway, and put his arms around me, slapping me on the back.

"Well, I never. Henry. I guess you got my letter then?"

I nodded.

"Well, come in, come in." He said, gesturing inside. "Hey, Belle, honey. We have a visitor. Could you fix some fresh coffee?"

I walked inside and found a heavily pregnant woman standing in the hallway. She was small, with medium length dark-brown hair and a welcoming smile on her face. "Hey, I'm Belle." She said, moving forward to shake my hand. "Henry." I told her.

Her expression changed to one of recognition and surprise. "Well, it's lovely to meet you, Henry. Now you go through to the living room with Ralph and I'll make us some refreshments."

"I don't want to put you to any trouble." I said, nodding toward her condition.

"I'm pregnant, not unable to move, honey." She laughed and waddled into the direction of what I presumed to be the kitchen.

I followed Ralph into the living room. "I'm sorry for turning up unexpectedly." I told him.

He shook me off. "Hey, we're not doing much these days other than relaxing and waiting for our daughter to appear. It's great to see you, son." He said. "But I'm guessing there's more to your visit than a reunion, boy?"

I sighed and then starting from the beginning I told him about me and Amelia.

He nodded throughout.

"You don't seem all that surprised about me and Amelia?" I questioned Ralph.

"I'm not, son, and I think you'll probably get the same response from Connie. Amelia's a determined young woman and Connie's found many a love heart drawn with your initials in it over the years. When she left supposedly to get a career in Manhattan, we knew she was on her way to find you. Connie's been waiting for the fallout, though she was expecting a brokenhearted Amelia returning home, rather than a romance, to be honest."

He patted my arm. "Now, with my sincerest apologies, what the hell are you doing here when you've left an emotional, pregnant woman at home? I know one thing. Connie finds that out and she'll kick your ass from here to Colorado, boy."

"Things were said. Amelia told me about a diary that said Vee didn't want the baby."

"Oh, fuck. I knew Connie should have burned that thing. I'm sorry you had to learn that, son."

"She was happy about the baby that morning. I know she was. That morning the baby had kicked. She said it was like it had suddenly all become real. That the baby in her stomach was alive, and a combination of the both of us and she got excited. She was bursting to tell you and Connie about it. Amelia was right about the house though. I had tried to be domineering and get Vee away from work, but also I'd moved near to the babysitter, Connie, the grandma-to-be. I knew we'd not keep Vee at home for long. I was having an office fitted, so she could work from home as much as possible and I'd planned to take a year off myself." I sighed. "Deep down if I admit it, I knew she wasn't ecstatic about the pregnancy. I just figured once she met the baby, it would all fall into place. A mother's love."

"I wish we'd known this, son. We've carried a lot of guilt around, thinking that your fairy tale wasn't exactly how you thought."

I sighed. "I am totally guilty after Vee's death of having painted my marriage as if it was faultless, when it was far from it. But I loved my wife desperately."

Belle walked in pushing a hostess trolley with coffee, iced-tea and a whole host of baked goods. "I like to cook, keeps me feeling productive." She explained.

I took a wonderfully smelling muffin from a plate. "Thank you, Belle. These smell delicious."

Ralph patted his toned stomach. "It's a good job we have the pool and the home gym, or I wouldn't be rocking this body at my age with Belle at home." He laughed.

"Yeah, well you've had quite the effect on my body!" Belle laughed, rubbing at her stomach. "Right I'm going to go water the plants while you men talk."

Despite my protests that it wasn't necessary she left us to it.

"You look really happy." I told Ralph.

"I am, son. Life's given me a do-over. Just like it's offering you one."

"I shouldn't be here, should I? I should be at home."

"There's only you who knows the answer to that question."

"Do you really think Connie will be pleased for us? She won't feel I've betrayed Vee's memory in some way?"

"I should expect she'll be delighted you've found happiness again, son. Not only that but she worried about Amelia. I think her being with you might alleviate some of those worries. There's not only you struggled since Vee died."

"I think before I go home, I'll call to see Connie. Do you have her cell number?"

So from Ralph's I drove on to Connie's house. I'd not been there since after the funeral. I pulled up in front of the front door and took a deep breath and stepped out of the car.

Connie's appearance shocked me. She looked twenty years older than when I'd last seen her, and I saw the years had not been kind with the loss of her daughter and worrying about Amelia. I felt guilty that I'd abandoned her, someone who I could have grieved with, someone who understood.

"I'm sorry I left and never came back." I told her. "So, damn sorry. Then I took Vee and Amelia's mom into my arms and the years fell away as we comforted each other.

Once again, I found myself in a living room being given a coffee.

"So you carried on with the property business. Still really successful?" She asked me.

"Yes, very."

"And the club?"

"Everyone seems to know about my secret club." I laughed.

"These things aren't so secret anymore, life's moving on and well, I'm feeling behind the times. Amelia makes me feel old with the things she talks about. All these reality shows where people have sex in front of the cameras. I'm old school, like to keep that kinda thing quiet."

I kept silent as I didn't know how to respond.

"Just tell me something, Henry. Are you happy working all those hours? Strikes me that you were all ready to give it up for the baby, then you became a workaholic, just like Vee."

I took a deep breath. "I thought I was continuing living, keeping busy. I realize now that what I'd actually done was immersed myself so deeply in work that I could pretend I was living, when really I was existing."

"And my Amelia, she's shown you that you're existing?"

My eyes met Connie's. "Yes." She has.

The reality hits me. As much as I've loved the buzz from business deals, I could walk away from it all tomorrow. All that was important to me now was Amelia and the baby. I'd move to the ends of the earth for them.

"Shit happens, Henry. And it's not true that lightning doesn't strike twice, but you can't live that way. It's not living. I know I was protective of Amelia, too much so, but when she said she was moving, she went with my blessing. She has her life to live and you have yours. You need to make a decision as to your future, Henry, and make it quick."

"I already made a decision," I told her. "That's one of the reasons I came here after seeing Ralph."

We spoke of what I hoped for the future and I saw tears spring to Connie's eyes. "Oh, Henry. I hope you'll both be very happy together and you'll have a beautiful, healthy child. I can't wait to be a grandma."

All I needed now was to drive back home, find Amelia, and beg her forgiveness.

"Oh, you don't need to drive home for that." Connie said. "Amelia's upstairs in her bedroom."

My mouth dropped open, "She's what?"

"Where do you think a girl's gonna go when she's pregnant and upset? She drove straight home to her mom."

CHAPTER THIRTEEN

Amelia

I should never have shouted those words in anger. They were Vee's secret, written in her diary and I had abused her trust, her memory, and destroyed Henry. The look on his face, the anger, misery, and disappointment, they would stay with me for a long time. I didn't want to face him when he returned. I felt he needed space away from me, and to be honest I needed space away from his suffocation. There was only one place to go. Home to my mom and dad.

The minute I'd walked through the door of my family home, I'd fallen into my mom's arms, broken down in tears, and told her everything. She'd done what my mom always did. Said everything would turn out as it was fated, and whether I ended up a single mom or we worked things out, she would look forward to being a grandma.

Then she told me something I never knew before. That when she'd met my dad, she'd known him years ago. She'd dated and been engaged to his best friend. It was way back before she'd married Ralph, but after they'd divorced her path had crossed with my father's again. "I could have said, oh it's not right, us dating after I dated your best friend, but life's short. Love is love."

I wiped another tear from my eye.

"Do you love Henry, sweetheart?"

"I do, Mom. I really do, and he loves me."

"Then that's all that matters. Now go have a lie down and then we'll see what needs to happen next."

And that's what I'd done. I'd come up to my old bedroom and crawled under the duvet where I'd fallen asleep. I'd woken up and stared around my bedroom wondering what on earth I would do next.

A soft knocking came on the door.

"Come in." I'd guessed it was my mom checking up on me. I didn't expect the door to open and Henry to walk through it.

He almost ran to my side.

"Henry, I-"

"No, me first. Please?"

I nodded.

"I've been a dick. A complete dick. I am so sorry. Once again, I'm wasting my precious life worrying about things that may never happen. I'm sorry, Amelia. Please come home. Let's work through things."

"I'm sorry too." I told him. "I should have been more understanding about your anxieties. I just felt a bit overwhelmed, you know? I've never been pregnant before, it's all new. I'm kinda a little scared about it all, anyway, and you just." I pulled a face. "Well, you were making it worse, suffocating me."

"I know. I realize that now. I can't pretend I'm suddenly going to become all laid back and chilled, because that's not me, but I will back off, or you can feel free to shout at me again."

"Henry, what I said about Vee. I'm so sorry."

"I already spoke to Ralph about this. I knew Vee wasn't happy." He continued to tell me the story of how the baby had kicked the morning Vee had died.

"There was no excuse for my behavior, regardless." I told him.

"Can we please draw a line under the whole thing and please go home?" He asked me.

"Yes," I nodded. "But could we stay to eat with my parents tonight first and then travel back?"

"Let's ask and if it's okay with them, we'll travel home in the morning and I'm going to spend the night seducing you in your teenage bed under your parents' roof."

And he did.

We were under the covers and I was trying so very hard not to moan in ecstasy as Henry tongued my clit.

"You taste divine. I think pregnancy has made your juices sweeter." He told me, staring up at me from between my thighs.

I stared at him through my lust-fueled haze. "Don't stop."

He kept on fluttering his tongue against my clit while he inserted two fingers inside me. I bucked against him.

"Oh, God," I moaned softly.

He moved back up the bed before I could come and spooning in behind me, he grabbed my hips and slid inside my heat, pulling me back against him and thrusting softly. The feeling was wonderful. We fit so well together.

His hand came around my front, carefully caressing my pregnancy sensitive nipples and breasts, and then fingers trailed down my front until he began strumming my clit alongside his thrusts from that oh so enormous cock I'd come to love. His movements came faster and my bed springs started to creak a little.

"Oh my god, how embarrassing." I told him.

He went back to slower thrusts, so the noise stopped. It was an agonizing pace and when my orgasm hit, I felt like I'd been rocked by an earthquake. I took Henry over with me, feeling his hot spurts of cum deep inside me.

We rested together until our breathing regularized and then fell asleep in each other's arms.

The next day before we left, we decided to visit Vee's grave. We stood in front and both bowed our heads deep in thought. Then Henry spoke.

"Veronica, I loved you with all my heart. If you're looking down on us, you'll see I hadn't been living my life since you left me. I'd like to think it was you, and your strategic business mind, that sent Amelia to me, so I could start living again. I'll never forget you, but now, I'm choosing to live."

Tears ran from my eyes. All I could manage to

say was, "Vee, I loved you so much. I miss you and I hope you are looking down, happy for us both."

Then Henry took my hand, we returned to the car, and he drove us home.

True to his word, Henry was much better from then on out. I agreed to regular health checks, more than I would usually receive, to keep him calmer, but as the pregnancy went along and especially after I got way past the date that Vee had, he slowly began to relax more.

I was six months pregnant when he (well, Mary), made us a picnic and said he was taking me to Central Park. The weather was mild, but not really picnic weather so we put on warm coats. He'd brought bacon sandwiches and hot coffee, and we sat on a bench in the park and enjoyed the food and drink.

"I'm selling the club." He told me. "To Aidan."

"You are? You don't have to on my account, you know? It's a good business."

"I don't want to be a dad and own a sex club. It doesn't feel right."

"Okay." I told him.

"Also, I was thinking of selling my property business to Eli King." Eli was another billionaire developer whose business was on the rise.

"So I'd work for Eli?" I said, tongue in cheek.

"Do you want to work for Eli?" He asked me. "Because you can. You can do whatever you want to do."

"I want to live with you and have many, many babies." I told him.

"Well, Eli discussed keeping me on in a consulting capacity. It means I can work the hours I want to work and can work from wherever we choose to live. Is there anywhere you'd want to go?"

I shook my head. "I like it here in Manhattan, but could we have a holiday home at The Hamptons? A small one? Maybe four-bedrooms, for us to grow into?"

Henry kissed my head. "Anything you want. You realize once you become Mrs. Carter you'll have my billions at your disposal, don't you?"

"Now who said anything about me becoming Mrs. Carter?" I narrowed my eyes at him.

Then he dropped to his knees. There in the park. Holding out a box containing the most beautiful ring.

"Amelia Ann Wilson. Would you do me the honor of becoming my wife?"

"Can we have the biggest, most elaborate

wedding ever, after I've given birth and had chance to slim down?"

"Anything."

"Like even have Justin Bieber sing at the reception?"

He laughed. "If he's available."

"Then, yes." I smiled.

"So it was Bieber that clinched it?" He winked.

"Yes, otherwise I'd have said thanks but no thanks," I joked.

He placed the band of diamonds on my finger. "I went for something non-traditional. I thought you wouldn't want anything that might dig into the baby's skin."

I looked at my beautiful ring. "It's perfect and thank you for thinking of that."

Then I fell to my own knees in the park and kissed my new fiancé while the people in New York walked and ran past us getting on with their day.

When we went home, Mary was in the kitchen preparing dinner. I flashed my diamond wearing finger at her.

"Oh my god," she squealed. "I'm so excited."

"We need to talk, Mary, about your post." Henry said, walking in behind me.

"Ah, I thought this day would be coming," Mary

said. "I know things will be changing now with the baby and everything."

"That's correct." Henry said, holding his serious business face in place and I could have killed him.

"Stop tormenting her." I scolded him. "Mary, we're staying here, but we're buying a home in The Hamptons too. Are you willing to travel, and also could we extend your duties to helping out with the baby, maybe babysitting sometimes, so me and my future husband can go on date nights?"

"Oh I'd be delighted. Thank you." She said, beaming widely.

Our baby chose that moment to kick. I held my hand to my belly.

"Looks like baby is delighted too." I told her.

CHAPTER FOURTEEN

Amelia

Lewis Henry Carter was born on the 23 March. He was a delight, and we were so very much in love with our baby boy. We waited a whole eighteen months, until he was toddling around, before tying the knot.

Our wedding was indeed a huge, elaborate affair, though by that time I'd gone off the Bieber idea and instead we had a band. The ceremony over and the reception underway, we made our way onto the dance floor for our first dance to John Legend's One Woman Man. He took me in his arms and held me tight.

"Thank you for bringing me back to life." He told me, capturing my mouth in his.

"Thank you for loving me and helping create our beautiful son." I replied.

As we danced, I noticed a white feather beside our feet on the dance floor. As the song ended, I picked it up and kissed it. I fully believed in white feathers being a sign from above and knew in that moment that my sister was giving us her blessing.

"Thank you, Vee, I love you." I whispered. Then I let go of the feather and watched it float back down to the dance floor as the other guests joined us to continue the celebrations.

THE END

Author note: H and Tiffany's story takes place in SOLD: Double Delights Book One.

Aidan Hall's story is next in The Billionaire and the Bartender: here

Read on for a sneak peek...

THE BILLIONAIRE AND THE
BARTENDER

Aidan

Partying with Henry Carter used to mean a threesome in his sex club. What a difference a year makes. Now we went out for a civilized meal and dragged fellow businessman, Elias King along with us. I'd been polite while H had shown us ten pictures of his son, Lewis, on his cell phone, but now he and Eli had launched into a full on conversation about having kids and I was bored as fuck.

"Hey. Can we talk about something else now, man? Your son's the most beautiful thing I ever saw but let's talk sports or some other shit."

Eli guffawed. "Oh, Aidan. You have all this to come."

"I really can't see it, not for me. I've met plenty of women I've liked well enough but the big old 'L' word, it's never happened to me."

Henry fixed me with a look and I knew what he was saying with that intense brooding gaze of his. A while ago we'd been talking about the deaths that had affected our pasts and I'd confessed that my brother had been killed in a motorcycle accident when I was fourteen. Henry had had to put his own tragic past behind him to be able to move forward with his now wife Amelia and I guessed he was hinting that my own past could be affecting my future. Or he could just be saying with that stare that I was a dick.

Elias took a drink of his scotch and then rubbed the spiky ends of his salt and pepper hair. We were quite a trio. Elias was forty-seven, the father of a twenty-four-year old daughter with a nightmare ex-wife who made the Housewives of New York look like sweet little puppies (yes, I'd caught an episode once). Actually, maybe it was that putting me off settling down here in Manhattan? Then there was Henry, who was forty; and me, the baby of the group at twenty-nine. Elias owned several businesses under his surname King, including residential properties, nightclubs, and a business school. I had the sex club I'd bought from Henry, and my adult movie company, GoDown Productions. Henry had sold everything apart from a house in Manhattan and one in The Hamptons and continued to work for Elias as a Consultant for his property business. I think the only thing he truly wanted to work on was having more babies with his wife these days.

"Out with it, Eli. When you rub that stubble we know there's something on your mind, old man."

He raised his middle finger at me.

"Just the one thing on your mind then?" I winked at him.

"My ex-wife is getting remarried."

"Hallefuckingluyah." I responded and Henry clapped.

"Yes, well she's getting married in January and she's decided that in the spirit of being amicable around our daughter that I've to attend and bring a plus-one." He rubbed his chin again. "Basically, she wants to show off that she's met a multi-billionaire who's better for her than I ever was."

"Just say you can't make it." Henry advised him. "If she's so madly in love she'll not even notice you're there."

"Brianna is putting the guilt on, 'Daddy, I never see you. It would be so nice if you and Mommy could finally put your differences aside'. I love my daughter but Christ she takes after her mother. She'll just want to hit me up for money and then I'll not hear from her again until her bank account runs dry once more."

Elias had told us the story of his bad marriage years ago. He'd fallen in love with whom he'd believed to be a sweet, lovely woman, but once the ring was on her finger and she'd gotten pregnant, she'd become a society climbing backstabber, who had to have the best of everything amongst her friends; an unrealistic ambition when some had royal connections. She'd basically made Eli's life a misery until she divorced him when their daughter was ten. He'd discovered she was having an affair with a Sheikh and had several properties in her portfolio that he'd not put there. It had been an ugly and messy divorce and she'd moved to Los Angeles, creating a distance between Eli and his daughter and making Brianna so spoiled that Eli despaired.

"You're gonna have to suck it up then and take a date with you. Preferably someone like twenty years younger than Katrina. No amount of plastic surgery is going to let her compete with a nubile young woman." I said.

Eli's face flushed. He picked up his scotch again and took a sip.

We talked business for a while and then Eli said. "Have any of you ever picked up any gossip about my assistant, Alexandra? You know, about her love life. Just, you know, I don't really like asking and she could have a celebration coming up, an engagement or similar. She's worked for me a few years now; it would be bad of me to miss such a thing."

"She's married, Eli, to the love of her life. Used to

be a fitness model." I joked with him and watched his face fall.

"Joking." I nudged him with my elbow. "Out with it. You have a crush on your assistant?"

He sighed. "No. I just had it pointed out to me that Alexandra might like me. I'm just working out if there's any basis to that."

"Who told you that?" Henry asked.

"Haley from Green's. She saw us together at a party a couple years ago."

"A couple of years ago? And you did nothing about it? Fuck, Eli. What's the matter with you?" I said exasperated.

"If Haley said it, I'd say there was probably some truth to it." Nodded Henry. "She's lovely, that girl. No mean side to her at all. So genuine."

"Yes, well I find it hard to believe seeing as I'm forty-eight and Alexandra is twenty-nine. My daughter is not much younger than her goddamn it."

"Well, Eli, I think you have your answer. The lovely Alexandra could be your plus-one to your ex-wife's wedding. If she hasn't given up all hope by now and joined a convent. All you have to do is find your balls and ask her." I shook my head at him.

Eli ordered another round of scotch.

"So, I hope I can count on you both to come to

the relaunch of the club next month?" I said. H's *Club S* would be no more. A complete redecoration was currently taking place and in two weeks time *Abandon* would be opening. I was excited. It was an entire new concept in sex clubs. There was a lot of competition in Manhattan of late and I wanted my club to be one of, if not THE best. There would be a high end movie theater showing GoDown's own movies of course. I was currently in negotiations about a line of sex toys that could be purchased and played with. I'd kept the black and silver tones of Club S, but the previous stage had now been removed from the bar area and would now become a relaxing zone where patrons could take a break if they so wished. Instead, there was a separate room containing a stage which could be hired and perfor- mances ran all night. All the staff at my club were strictly off limits and in order to enforce that rule I'd decided that I would no longer take part now I owned the place, taking on the mantra of 'don't shit where you eat'. This would seriously affect my sex life, but I was sure I'd find someone to hook up with should the need arise, and I could always grab the number of a sexy woman from the club. Finally, there would be a series of rooms, all fitted with windows with blinds, in case people wished to be watched or keep their fantasies private. All rooms however were fitted with security cameras and I had a team on board to make sure that everyone played safe.

"Yes, Amelia can't wait for an evening out. She says we might visit one of the rooms to play so I'm definitely attending." H said.

"Good to see the support for your fellow businessman." I quipped.

"He's pussy whipped or wants the opportunity to whip the pussy. You selling whips?" Eli chuckled. "Anyway, I'll be there. Purely to see your up and running empire. I won't be partaking. No offense but sex in public just isn't my thing."

"No offense taken, old man. There's no one wants to see your wrinkly dick." I laughed.

"I think a whip needs taking to your ass, boy, only not in a sexual way. Don't cheek your elders." A small smirk curled the edge of Eli's top lip.

"Why don't you bring Alexandra with you to the launch? See what she thinks to it?"

"Not a cat in hell's chance. I'll be flying solo that night."

"Pussy."

"Yes, I should imagine I'll see lots of it."

He patted Henry on the back. "I think we should

look around, H, and see if we can't find a woman for our Aidan here. He needs someone to keep him in line, don'tcha think?"

"It'll happen to him when he's least expecting it." H replied.

I shook my head. "No way. I'm still young. No intention of settling down any time soon. I'm still empire building. No woman will want to be stuck at home while I'm out at my sex club."

"Why would they be stuck at home?" Eli queried.

"I wouldn't want any woman of mine hanging round that kind of establishment. They might decide they want a threesome. We know there's plenty of those around," I said to H, as we used to take part in a hell of a lot of threesomes to make women's fantasies come true at Club S.

"You hypocrite! You mean after all you've taken part in, in the past, you want a woman all to your-self?" H's jaw dropped.

"Absofuckinglutely. I refuse to share my woman's pussy with anyone. In fact I'm going to fit her with a pussy lock when I find her."

Eli and Henry guffawed.

"Oh my god, you are crazy. Fucked up crazy. So your ideal woman is what? A sex-crazed stunner who's willing to wear a chastity belt and stay at home while you mingle with women who want to have threesomes with you?"

"That's about it, yes."

More laughter ensued. "Then there's no wonder you are still fucking single." H said.

Eli's cell beeped. He picked it up, and a smile played out on his face. He typed out a quick message. When he put his cell back on the table, we were both staring at him.

"Who was that?" I asked.

Eli cleared his throat. "It was Alexandra. She sends me a text when she's home."

"Excuse me?" H said. "Want to run that past us again?"

"Look, I can't even remember how it started, but we must have been on a working dinner or something and I asked her to text me when she got home safely, and she laughed and said I had to text her too and then she kept on with it. She texts me every night and I do the same. It's nothing. Just lets someone know you're home safely, like a security thing."

"Oh dear god, are you really that stupid, Eli? You like this woman and by the sounds of it, she likes you."

"She's far too good an assistant for me to fuck it up by fucking her."

"Okay, whatever you say, Eli, but I think you're being a complete dick and ought to grow a pair of balls." I huffed at him in frustration.

H sat back and looked at both of us. "I don't know which of you is dumber. The one who won't take a chance on his assistant because she's great at her job, bearing in mind, Manhattan is full of amazing PA's, or the guy who thinks he can own a sex club and his wife will just sit at home and cook his dinner. It comes to something when I've become the most well-adjusted out of the three of us."

He had a point.

"I will find myself a woman. Just to shut you all up. I will find that very woman. Who will let me own her pussy all by myself and accept my job."

"Okay, and when are you going to find her by, because this sounds like something to wager on." H said.

"At the very latest by Christmas."

"Three months? You're going to find the woman of your dreams in three months?" Eli shook his head.

"At the latest. You know me. I love a challenge."

"So what's the wager?" H asked.

"If I lose, I'll babysit your daughter once a week.

If you lose you are only allowed to show me pics of the kids at their birthday and at Christmas, with a maximum allotted time of five minutes exactly."

"You have no heart, but deal." H said.

"Eli. If I win, you have to ask your assistant out. What do you want if I lose?"

"You take my nightmare of a daughter out and somehow try to make her human."

"Holy crap. I'd better make sure I win." I said and shook Eli's hand.

Then we carried on drinking scotch and shooting the breeze until it was time to head off home.

Angel Devlin is the sexy alter-ego of paranormal, rom com, and suspense writer, Andie M. Long.

She lives in Sheffield with her partner, son, and a gorgeous whippet called Bella.

Angel Devlin

His Perfect Martini

Santa's Christmas Cracker

Love and Liquor Series

Banned

Lucked

Double Delight Series

Sold

Submit

Share

Box set available

The Billionaires Series

The Billionaire and the Virgin

The Billionaire and the Bartender

The Billionaire and the Assistant

Box set available

Abandon Series

Abandon

School of Seduction Series

Rule Him

Teach Me

Sign up to Angel's newsletter

here

Made in the USA
Columbia, SC
18 April 2022

59156617R00098